THE HAUNTING OF PASTOR BUTCH GREGORY

AND OTHER STORIES

Jamie Greening

ATHANATOS
PUBLISHING GROUP

The Haunting of Pastor Butch Gregory And Other Stories

By Jamie Greening

www.divinehaunting.com

Published by Athanatos Publishing Group

www.athanatosministries.org

ISBN: 978-0-9822776-6-9

Illustrations by Kim Wells Greening

Cover by Angela Eldridge

Table of Contents

Acknowledgements

It is cliché, but there are so many people to thank that I could never name them all. However, there are some which must be named. Tony Horvath at Athanatos Christian Ministries has my deepest gratitude for giving this book a chance. Bonnie Stancikas and Sarah Rice-McDaniel worked tirelessly in helping me get the manuscript polished. Dirk Jackson was a major encouragement to me in the creative endeavor.

There are three churches which have contributed to me as a fully actualized human being and a minister and therefore this book would have been impossible without them. I grew up in First Baptist Church, Hughes Springs, Texas. It was the first community of faith I ever identified with and will forever be near to my heart. Walnut Springs Baptist Church in Walnut Springs, Texas is the place where I learned the craft of my calling through trial and error. Sadly it was mostly error as I distinctly remember blundering through one mistake after another. Finally, First Baptist Church, Port Orchard, Washington has walked with me for over ten years in the ups and downs, ins and outs, of life together. They truly are the greatest congregation on the planet—many thanks.

Most of all, I would like to thank the women in my life. In my formative years it was my mother who demonstrated to me that reading was something to enjoy, not a chore to finish. My two daughters, Chelsea and Phoebe, teach me more than I could ever teach them. Kim Greening, my wife and best friend, has not only lovingly read everything I've ever written but also is the best proof reader in the world, not to mention a great sketch artist. Without her love, nurture, and encouragement, I would be helpless.

Foreword

On one hand, writing about the church is easy. It is easy because it is what I know. I grew up in the church and have lived in a church environment since I was seven years old. I know when church is good, bad, and ugly. I've seen it all. On the other hand, writing about the church is hard. I have spent my life serving the Kingdom of God through her and I want what is best for her. Hurting her is never in view.

That is why this is a fiction book. Nothing in here is a blow-by-blow telling of any one event (Well, except *Who Flushed*. That story happened almost exactly as I wrote it.) What I have done instead is compiled various thoughts, trends, or occurrences in a fictional format which attempts to convey some of the nature of pastoral ministry. I am not writing so much about the church itself as I am describing my own vocation within the church. Butch Gregory's emotions, turmoil, and fears reflect those I've heard from many different ministers. *Legacy* is not meant to attack any leader's motives, but instead is a parody designed to make us think about the way we are tearing at each other. Truthfully, I lampoon only those whom I respect deeply.

Fiction means it is made up, but it doesn't necessarily mean it is not true. In that way, therefore, every story in here is true. Actually, these stories might be truer than some non-fiction which is on my bookshelf.

"What is truth?" a cynic once asked.

The truth is that pastors, clergy, and spiritual leaders of all types view the world differently than most everyone else. For us, the world is filled with large masses of people who are in need of help and comfort. At the same time, we see the world filled with the unseen hand of God working in all situations in some mystical way we can never fully comprehend. This bifocal vision of reality puts enormous strain on the spirituality of the minister.

The truth is that pastoral ministry is hard. The difficulty comes from two different directions. The first is the internal pressure to live up to the calling we know we have. Men and women who are serving the Lord with integrity will go to bed every night knowing there was so much left undone, but also knowing all of it will never get done. The second pressure is external. All people have different expectations of the minister which force him or her to conform to differing roles. One minute the pastor is the communicator. The next she is a theologian, the next a grief counselor, and then suddenly an administrator. No one in the world is competent in all of these different fields, yet the pastor is expected to be. This makes the church a very frustrating place to live and an exacting boss.

The truth is that pastors have fallen on hard times. Changes in what it means to be a church or to do church have inevitably created great strain on the psyche of ministers. No one really knows what to do anymore. Everyone has done what is right in their own eyes. The result is that no uniform pattern exists for what is expected of those doing pastoral ministry. There are no models to work from, except mega-church rock star pastors, but these are unrealistic and impractical. The irony of it all is that the most famous 'pastors' in America don't really pastor anyone in anything close to the biblical and historical setting of a local church. I would like to indicate, for the record, that I believe there is nothing wrong with the mega-church model or the superstar pastors who lead them. Our world needs high profile pastors, our age demands it. My argument is that their existence is so unfamiliar to the everyday life of most ministers that they provide no working model to go by. As much as I admire Bill Hybels; his world is not my world.

The truth is pastors have been sold a false bill of goods. For the last twenty years it has been preached to us by our denominations and the important people of the ecclesiastical world that success is marked by building the church bigger, richer, and more significant. This bigger, faster, stronger motif has undermined the difficult work of shepherding souls in the ways of the Lord. There is nothing wrong with being a big church, a rich church, or a significant church. I want my church to be all three of those. However, these man-made litmus tests of wealth and power are not success. Successful ministry is nothing less and nothing more than the one who remains faithful to the Lord who called.

As strong as these truths are, there are truths which are greater still.

The greater truth is that the Lord has called men and women to work in the vineyards of this planet. These local church vineyards are where the real action of ministry is. The real action is discipleship, ministry to those in need, preaching, and worship. The men and women who till and prune in these vineyards are doing what only they can do because only they have been called to do it. These individuals will never be famous nor have buildings named after them, at least not on this side of eternity.

The greater truth is that with the ministerial milieu melting down around us, the Lord is reshaping his church. Our time of upheaval will come and go and the fads of the land will fade. What will be left are stronger pastors who will return toward the classical, millennia tested work of devotion, prayer, the word, and worship. We know this is true because this is what history teaches us always happens.

The greater truth is there is no work on the planet more fulfilling or rewarding than pastoral ministry. The difficulties involved are the precise things which make it so meaningful. Helping churches hit on all cylinders, leading souls into a relationship with God through Christ, and teaching faithfully the Bible to people who do know what it says or means, is the pinnacle of what "thrill" means.

The greater truth is one of neediness. The western world needs pastors now more than ever. We are painfully learning that psychology, medicine, self-help, and government cannot do what needs to be done to help people. The spiritual side of the human composition has been so neglected. As we emerge from our over-dependence on science the craving for authentic spirituality will be great. People will reject the false because it is evidently false. Eventually they will return again to the Way. When that happens, it will be pastors who will lead the way like the priests leading across the Jordan.

The greatest truth of all is that Jesus Christ is Lord. In his wisdom he has chosen the weak vessels of human beings to be the living and breathing ambassadors for the gospel. In the human frailty of the pastor's life, God's strength is made manifest. This is the plan which has worked since the church was born on Pentecost, and it is the plan which Christ is still using today. We do not know what we are doing, but he certainly knows exactly what he is doing.

Soli Deo Gloria
Jamie Greening
Ash Wednesday, 2010

The Haunting of Pastor Butch Gregory

It was right where he left it.

It is always a good feeling when something is found exactly where it is expected. He expected it to be sitting there on the long folding table in the vast hallway. He had left it there the night before. The night before, just eleven hours ago, when he had turned off the lights, turned off the heat, and placed his old half-filled coffee cup on the table. He was truly surprised to see his coffee cup there because the more familiar feeling is to never find anything where it is expected.

He had left it there last night because he didn't want to walk back out to his study, and his hands were too full to put it in the kitchen.

It spent the night right where he put it.

The mug was like him. On the outside was a picture of bright daisies yellow against a green field with a verse about Jesus being the way, the truth, and the life. But on the inside it was all brown, stained with years of very strong coffee. It truly was a perfect metaphor for his life: cheery and happy on the outside for the world to see yet dark and stained (or maybe strained, he thought out loud) on the inside from years of worry and struggle trying to keep the caffeine flowing to give the church a shot of energy. He thought there was Bible truth in there somewhere— whitewashed coffee cups, he chuckled to himself. That might just preach. He would have to write that down in his little black book of sermon ideas and other miscellany.

He felt especially stained this morning. Monday morning. It was a dreaded cycle which repeated itself every week of his life. For most of the free world, Monday is the first day of the week. There is an understandable drain on most people about the thoughts of going back to work. He understood that. But what he felt every Monday was different. It was psychic. It was emotive. It was physical. But most of all, it was spiritual.

Monday was not the first day of the workweek. For Pastor Butch Gregory, Monday was the second day of his cyclic labor. His first day had been yesterday. Sunday was the big show, and he had to be on his game. If he wasn't, it could mean disaster. He even knew of some in his calling for whom a few bad Sundays strung together resulted in a long board meeting that ended in someone getting fired, and it was never the board which was fired. Butch kept that pressure always in the back of his mind. Sundays he had to be at least good, and if possible, great.

His family's financial well-being depended on him performing to the church's satisfaction. An unfortunate reality, but experience had taught him it was cold, hard fact.

Fortunately, most Sundays Butch was at least good enough. This Monday morning he felt particularly good about yesterday's sermon. It had pieced together quite a bit of biblical literature ranging from the Patriarchs to the Apostles as well as pop culture. He had argued for a connection between Joseph, Paul, and Chuck Colson in their prison experiences. He had likened it to a beluga whale he had seen at the aquarium.

The majestic white whale had caught his eye, and the two made eye contact—mammal to mammal, Ahab to Moby. In the whale's eye Butch thought he caught a glimmer of sad resignation. The whale seemed to know the rest of her life would be spent in captivity. A beast meant to frolic in the frigid seas was now being hand fed, spending its time pushing around a red ball while swimming in a giant pool. God had made the behemoth to swim the depths of the ocean and live in the depth of mystery humanity would never know. We had stolen that destiny from the whale and cast her in prison.

Butch told his congregation that we were the same way, except our prisons were made of our own doing. "The shackles binding us," he'd said, "were poor choices, negative thinking, and a haunting past." He had told them, "God did not make us like that. God made us to be free and to swim the depths and mysteries of life. Jesus came to free us," he said. He believed it.

It was a good sermon. He would keep it in his files.

But that was yesterday. This was Monday.

This Monday morning he felt not so much like a prisoner as much as a fatigued athlete in need of a breather. Perhaps someone should invent a tag-team ministry model where Sunday and Monday can be rotated out. Over his twenty years in the ministry he had tried to explain the Monday drain feeling to his friends in secular jobs, but they didn't understand. Only someone in his shoes could understand the drain. Sunday eats energy; to get up and preach three services, then to smile,

2

hug, counsel, hear with empathy the grieving mother, the story about the young dad with cancer, to pray over the amputee, and talk the couple out of filing for divorce.

On top of these issues there were grumbling musicians and sound people. He always had to convince the sound people that he did know what he was doing. Sound people seemed to be the worst to communicate with. There must be a Grand Secret Society of Church Sound Booth Engineers (the GSSOCSBE maybe?) who have put together a manual on everything sound people need in order to make a preacher's life as painful as possible. Then there was always the work of soothing out the discord over shared classroom space with teachers, making sure the guests had been meeted and greeted, announce all the announcements, and remember to recognize the Bohannons on their golden wedding anniversary.

Every colleague he'd known felt the same way about Mondays. Most of them took Monday off because of the drain. They played golf. They read. They slept in. They did the crossword. Butch had tried that early on, when he was a young pastor, but he still felt the drain. The drain ruined his golf swing. The drain distracted his reading. The drain woke him up early anyway. He eventually decided that if he was going to feel bad anyway, he might as well get work done and take Friday off instead. That way he would feel better on his time and not the church's time.

Settling In

Here it was, Monday morning and the drain was doing its work. It was exactly 8:03 A.M. It had taken him thirteen minutes to get to the building from the middle school parking lot where he had dropped off his oldest daughter. It used to take nine minutes, but traffic had picked up in the last couple of years to the extent that it cost him four more minutes of drive time. He would pick her up in the afternoon.

Grabbing his coffee cup he walked into the kitchen, dropped his satchel on the table, and made the coffee. He had learned to make the coffee strong in this Navy town. The Northwest was famous for its designer lattes and mocha madness; but in this no-nonsense blue collar Seattle satellite, plain-Jane dripped coffee was king. He had gotten used to it and wore a certain badge of honor that he was able to avoid the ridicule of drinking foofoo coffee by the crusty old men he called friends.

"Were they really friends?" he asked himself. The question mocked him there under the fluorescent kitchen light.

He guessed so. They were the closest things to friends he had. Except for his wife, no one really knew him; at least not as a person. He was only a title, a figurehead, a commodity. They rarely called him by his name. In social settings he was only introduced as, "This is our pastor." They even did this to his wife; "This is our pastor's wife." He was always just a title. They never asked him how he was doing. It was always all about them and what they wanted him to do or say or be. Prayer was a one way street. Always giving, never receiving. Jesus had said it was better to give than to receive, but that didn't keep the hurt from welling up inside.

The drain was getting to him today. He didn't want to feel this way. He knew it was wrong.

Butch also knew he had to shake it off. "Shake it off Gregory, shake it off," he said as he smiled. The benefit of experience is that he recognized what was happening and knew how to correct it.

The coffee brewed quickly in the Bunn and he filled his coffee cup, grabbed his satchel and walked out to the administration building where his study was. He darted through the rainy walkway, unlocked the door, and punched in the secret code on the alarm pad. Some secret he thought. Half the church knew the code. If they were ever burglarized every church member would be a suspect.

Briskly he walked down the hallway to his study.

Butch then did what he had done nearly ever morning since he was ten years old. He talked to Jesus.

He opened up his prayer book and prayed the words. "Alleluia! Christ is risen. The Lord is risen indeed. Alleluia!" It was Monday, so he really needed these words. His devotions today moved him to contemplate the spring season and how death really did always give way to life. Doubt eventually has to give way to faith. Hate must be overtaken by love. It just has to be.

Christ is risen indeed.

Soon Butch was on his knees saying the penitential prayer. Being on his knees helped him stay focused upon his neediness. He was only a man. He was a broken man. The Bible taught he was a sinful and fallible man. On Mondays he believed it more than other days.

Years ago when he was a young buck preacher bent on changing the whole world all by himself, he had thought he was superman. He thought he was able to do anything: save souls, wax poetic, administer the budget, and comfort the hurting all before dinner and still have plenty left to give his wife and children at home. As he had grown older he knew better. He was far from superman. He was nothingman. He couldn't save anyone. His poetry was trite. The budget was always off. The hurting kept choosing the "First Church of Where It's At" down the street with the multimillion dollar worship facility and the television ministry. Apparently, hurting people are helped more by glitz and high definition screens.

These thoughts crept into his mind as he still knelt there on the floor. When they had come and gone, he now needed to confess the sin of bitterness and envy. These would add nicely to his usual confession of guilt and shame; pride and prejudice, or any other Jane Austen titles. What else should he confess while he was down here? Lust—no, no lust today. Too tired. Greed—no greed today. Hate—no hate today, wait, yes, Lord forgive me for hating the guy who always falls asleep before I have even read the morning text. Narcolepsy was a terrible bitter root for him.

He confessed all of this out loud. He didn't look up. He looked down with his glasses laying on top of his prayer book. Then from memory he repeated the scripted words:

I have sinned against you in thought, word, and deed.
By what I have done, and by what I have left undone.
I have not loved you with my whole heart,
and I have not loved my neighbor as myself.

It comforted him that perhaps millions of people around the globe were praying something similar too this morning. Because we are all nothingmen and nothingwomen.

He then read his Psalm and moved quickly to the Old Testament reading. It was from the old histories of Ancient Israel. His world seemed so distant from the bloodshed and strange cultic practices of the Yahwists. Except today. His reading was about King David near the

5

end of his life. For some reason he decided to take a census of all the people in Israel. He probably wasn't asking how many toilets they had.

Why count the people? It wasn't very Hebrew to count your numbers. It was more Roman. It was so non-Hebrew that it made God mad and he punished David severely.

This problem pounded Butch in his frontal lobe. Last week he had finished reading a book given him by his denominational leader which was all about how to accurately count all the people involved in the ministries of the church. He had liked the book and given it to a man in his church to implement. He had told his deacon, "We need to do this so we know where we're at and how effective we are."

That was his reasoning.

That is the reasoning which was given to him by the well-meaning denominational leader.

But now reading David's destructive arithmetic made him wonder. Did we need to do this? Why? Who cares how many? Isn't it more important to be faithful? Is counting all these things more about keeping the denomination happy and the money flowing and the press releases positive than anything which God really cares about? If we do the right things, then they are the right things regardless of the numbers.

It was here he decided, as he stared at the page with the old story on it, that the church was just as guilty as David. The church growth gurus were leading pastors down a particular kind of idolatry to worship the purpose driven golden calf. What was indeed emerging in the church was the whore of Babylon. When David trusted strategies it got him trouble but when he trusted in God it got him God's grace.

Again, Butch arrested the thought process.

The bile seemed so close to the surface today. None of what he had just thought was true.

He was taking David out of context.

It was just Monday and on Monday morning he always hated the church. That is why he keeps a resignation letter in his desk drawer. Today, the Monday drain seemed acerbic. Had he been of the sort to blame, "the devil behind every bush," he would have blamed the evil one. However, Butch knew it was not the devil. It was him. Ministry was just hard. Life was hard. He was weak.

He turned to his New Testament reading from the gospel. It didn't help him much, but at least he did find a compatriot in suffering. The text was Jesus lamenting over Jerusalem. Christ wanted to gather the bitter city like a hen gathers chicks. Christ wept over the brokenness of his chosen people.

Butch decided this must have happened to Jesus on a Monday morning.

His devotional now followed with a recitation of the creed and the Lord's Prayer. He prayed for his flock and said his, "Amen." He felt better. He had talked to Jesus and it seemed like Jesus understood his burden. The burden wasn't gone but it became tolerable. He glanced across his desk. It was 9:00 A.M. The rest of his small staff would be in the office now and it was time for the weekly ritual of schedule alignment, propaganda materials, crisis management, and trying to figure out the next six days.

He thought about a quick check of his email to see if the magazine he sent that sermon to had responded yet. It was on the East Coast and perhaps a Monday morning reply had been shot out. He was on the verge of giving up on it. No one really cared about local stuff and real people. It had to be in Nashville or Atlanta or some other hub of holiness to matter. Colorado seemed about as far west as ecclesiastical significance could go.

"But they may say yes," he said aloud to no one. That acceptance email just might be there, but he also knew he would find in his inbox the usual two or three complaining emails. These complaining emails were like modern imprecatory psalms in which his parishioners wished to dash his sermonic babies against the rocks. One would probably complain that he hadn't worn a necktie yesterday morning. The other would complain the music was too loud, too slow, too fast, too much or too little. Then another might be that enough attention was not given to women's ministry.

Inexplicably and suddenly the image of the beluga whale came into his mind. The whale he had preached about yesterday; the whale held captive by the whims of others. He could see the whale swimming around in circles looking for a way out of the fishbowl she was stuck in.

He would not check his email. That would keep him free from hurt for at least a little while. It was time for staff meeting.

The Mundane

The highlight of the staff meeting was a protracted discussion about the phones. A well meaning deacon had installed a new phone system with all new phones. The problem was the phones in the individual offices didn't seem to like each other. Butch wondered if one phone was a Methodist, one was Assembly, one was Catholic and the rest were Non-Denominational. Individually each of the phones worked just fine, but they just couldn't get along very well. Calls could not be transferred from one line to another and people put on hold would get cut off. The intercom feature did not work either, except for that one hour window last Wednesday when it blinked into existence, but then blinked out.

Yep. Just like different denominations. But maybe one was Lutheran and not Assemblies. Butch was pretty sure an Assemblies phone would be able to talk to everyone in all kinds of languages.

The Secretary, a kind woman named Mildred, said she didn't understand why this problem even existed. Neither did Butch nor Brian, his associate, or Selena the youth pastor. The root problem then came out into the open. The deacon who built the system was now gone on a business trip for five weeks. This left the beleaguered ministers two options. Option one was to call a professional to come fix it. This was the obvious and most reasonable option. The problem is it would cost money and thereby infuriate the treasurer and no one wanted to deal with him. It would also hurt the feelings of the beloved deacon they all liked. Therefore, they settled in on option two. Option two was to continue to yell down the hallway at each other whenever a phone call was for someone else. They would do this until the deacon returned from his trip and fixed the problem.

They had done this all last week and it was funny at first. "Miss Fanny on line 2 Butch, she is going in tomorrow for a fungus check."

"Brian, your 3:30 sex addict is on line 4."

"There's a missions moment on line 1, Mildred, for the newsletter."

"Selena, you've got a troubled homeless teen needing a pregnancy test on line 3."

Of course this had been happening all week, with people coming in and out of the building wondering exactly what their staff was doing. Butch had almost recommended that the church get rid of the phones altogether and publish cell phone numbers. It would be cheaper and much more logical. Of course, for that reason alone it would never fly, never be approved. Churches were never logical. Ever. Plus, most of them already had his cell number and called at the most inopportune times.

The second big issue of the staff meeting was what to do with Ricky. Ricky lived next door to the facility and had wandered in about three weeks ago. He said he needed to do 2000 hours of community service and that since he lived next door to the church he figured that would be easiest for him. It, however, was not easier for the church.

As soon as Mildred had agreed to let him do his community service, Ricky began listing things he couldn't do. He couldn't lift because of a bad back. He couldn't walk much because of a bad knee. He couldn't work back to back hours because of his medication. He couldn't handle heights. Ricky defined heights as anything over 1 foot.

Over the past three weeks Butch had learned just exactly how long 2000 hours are. Ricky had done the crime, but his staff was doing the time. Ricky kept telling Mildred how to do her job, argued with Brian, and had the nasty habit of barging into Butch's study at the exact moment when he was just on the verge of a great insight. Last Wednesday Butch was pretty sure he had almost solved the Free Will/Predestination debate which had raged for centuries in Christianity but Ricky came in and interrupted his flow of thought. Now it was gone forever.

Mildred wanted to send him away. Selena thought he was cool in a grifters kind of way. Brian voted for compassion and reformation— maybe Ricky would give his heart to Christ. Butch was more cynical. He feared if Ricky were sent away he might burn the building down or throw rocks through the stained glass. He figured his back and knee wouldn't stop him from doing that.

In the end they decided to endure the 2000 hours as the cross they would bear. Butch decided to pray Ricky violate his probation and get sent to jail. That would make the problem go away. But then he was afraid he'd have to visit him behind the glass wall. Butch shuddered. It was truly a no win situation.

Selena brought up her recent problem at the youth lock-in. Butch hated lock-ins because it seemed nothing good ever came from them. His hypothesis was about to be confirmed. Selena had found Randi and

Misty kissing behind the couch. Before he had heard the whole report, Butch said, "Just do what you always do, remind them that PDA is not appropriate at church events, give them a warning and tell them if it happens again you'll tell their parents."

Butch felt smug because he had settled it so quickly and efficiently.

Selena cleared her throat and said, "Excuse me, Dr. Gregory," Butch was wary because his staff never called him by his honorific unless he had just made a mistake. Selena continued, "Randi is a girl."

Butch sat a moment before it hit him. Oh how his world had changed. None of this was covered in his seminary classes.

Throughout the past years Butch had wanted to be sensitive to the changing world and had no desire to be the sex police, although his view of sexuality was very conservative. These types of things were like napalm. It scorched everything. After much conversation, eventually they all agreed to treat it the same way they would have treated a guy-girl thing, except with a direct talk to both of them about the Bible's words regarding homosexuality.

Mildred was silent, but it was clear she didn't approve. Butch assumed she wanted a full blown church meeting on the issue. Mildred did not have a tolerant bone in her body. Yet, it wasn't her call to make. It was his and he knew that teens are confused enough as it is.

Staff meeting ended with a collective trip to the coffee pot. That is the way it always ended. As Butch entered the main building he found a woman he had never seen before standing in the hallway. She looked worn and dirty. Her face was lined with a million lines and her eyes did not have crow's feet, they had crow's legs. Her hair was a stringy tangled mess of gray and blonde. Her eyes were jaundiced and sallow. She smiled at him with the saddest grin which flashed the lone gold tooth in her head.

Butch asked the question but he already knew the answer. "May I help you?" Brian was standing behind him. Mildred just turned and walked the other way. She deplored these folks more than she liked coffee. Selena had magically disappeared.

The gold toothed woman said meekly, "St. Vinny's said you had food."

He was right again.

The church operated a modest food pantry. People from the

congregation gave green beans, mac and cheese, cereal, and other staples. Anyone who wanted food could get it, no questions asked. The problem with the system was staring Butch in the face with her vacant stare. The church's intentions were to help those in need who perhaps didn't have enough to tide them over until payday, minimum wage workers, the one time crisis, or the many with medical issues. Yet the food pantry had turned into an enabler of drug addicts.

It did not take a detective of Sherlock Holmes capacity to determine that this woman was a meth addict. Many meth addicts came through. They were easy to spot with their thin wispy frames, bad teeth, and vacant glare. This woman was even tweeking here in the church hallway under the silver chandelier. Her nervous twitch and shake betrayed her attempts to look okay.

It wasn't always meth. Sometimes it was just plain old alcohol. There was always a cigarette smell. Usually a terrible body odor went along with them. That is why Butch had begun putting bars of soap and other toiletries in the food bags.

Butch and most of the other folks in his parish could easily walk away from helping folks like this. The reason they didn't, wouldn't, and couldn't was the kids. There were always children involved; sometimes they were in the backseat of the cars when he would take the food out. They would look up at him and stare a silent plea for help. Their clothes were always dirty and their diapers needed changing. Little soiled bodies sadly scrawny and malnourished. He always helped addicts because it wasn't the children's fault.

As Butch took the food out to the woman's beat up Ford Tempo he spied two children in the backseat. He guessed their ages 4 and 5. They were too young for school, so they didn't get free lunches and breakfast. He smiled at them and said hi. They didn't respond. They both just gazed at him from behind the glass door window.

"Jesus loves you," he told the woman. He again smiled at the children. He wished he had a candy bar to give them or soda. She looked back and said, "Do you have any milk?"

"No." He answered quickly because he had been asked the same question a million times. "Milk goes bad. We can't keep it. There is some powdered milk in the bag. I wish I could do more."

That was true. He wished he could do more and he would start by taking her kids away from her. He thought of two infertile couples he knew who would love to take in a couple of children if possible, no questions asked.

He walked away. About halfway to the front door he glanced back at the car and again eyeballed the two children in the backseat. The car was a prison for them. It kept them chained to a miserable, warped existence apart from the world of joy where normal boys and girls sleep in a clean bed at night and eat oatmeal in the mornings. As he stared at them, he noticed they were still looking at him.

The image of the beluga whale again psychically shimmered through his thoughts. These children were imprisoned by the choices they did not make. They were held hostage and captive by the evil of their parents. Why was it true—why God? Why was it true that the sins of the fathers are visited upon the children to the third and fourth generation? Why?

"Jesus, make it stop," he mumbled as a prayer. At least the whales were well fed and certainly got good medical attention. The same could not be certain for these two precious children created in the image of God.

Walking back into the building he remembered what he had come over here to do. He picked up the same stained daisy field coffee cup where he had put it, on the hallway table just like last night and headed toward the kitchen. Someone had made a fresh pot and he was thankful—he sang a little doxology in his heart,

"Praise God from whom all java flows,
praise him all baristas here below,
praise him above ye dark roast,
praise Father Son and Holy Ghost. Amen."

Butch thought his praise might be heretical, but probably not. Do not the Scriptures say to give thanks in all things? Certainly anything as beautiful as coffee was worthy of giving thanks.

He glanced at his watch. It was 10:26. "D—" the word almost slipped. He almost swore, but stifled it like one aborts a sneeze in mid "ah" just before the "choo." He had worked very hard on swearing since he preached about it about six months ago. He feared being a hypocrite.

It is a myth that ministers don't swear. They do. The only difference is they have to watch it. It is a little known secret that some ministers curse aggressively, especially when around other ministers. But Butch had earnestly tried to curtail this humanity.

Grinning, he realized he embodied a thought—praise one minute, profanity the next. The Apostle James had something to say about that. He thought about the famous pastor over in Seattle with the megachurch who was proud of his swearing. Butch, though, still thought holiness was something to be strived for, even if it was unattainable and unhip.

What had brought him to the point of swearing was the time. In four minutes he had yet another meeting. He was completely unprepared for it because he had planned to use the half hour after staff. But that half-hour was taken with gold toothed meth addict and neglected children.

This meeting he was walking into was about children. They were to plan a summer children's ministry with the lay leadership team. He wondered what would happen if he brought up the meth addict with the neglected children in his ministry team meeting. Could they really do anything to help people in that situation? Did anything they do really matter? Would it make a difference in the lives of any children?

He poured his coffee. He rushed to his study. He beat out an agenda from memory of the exact same meeting last year. Butch clicked print then speedily walked down the hallway to the printer. He snatched the agenda, made copies and walked into the conference room. The ministry team was waiting for him. It was 10:33.

"You are late," a middle aged woman snapped at him.

"My apologies, I was detained with an urgent issue."

"More urgent than children?" the middle aged woman retorted. She glared at him with an air of religious righteous superiority. Butch hated that glare, but he let it go. He almost mentioned the meth addict and the neglected children. No. That would be too much. A first aid kit is not enough to treat cancer. What they were doing was important. But it wasn't the solution to the world's problems. He would have to remember that thought the next time he reckons about big things. Right now, he just had a hard time shaking that terrible feeling of impotence. He also had to shake off his anger toward the middle aged woman. She just didn't know what she didn't know.

This Monday was tough.

But they all were.

The leader of the team talked about the event planned and the theme. The theme was "Island Paradise." As she talked, Butch daydreamed a bit. He thought of a warm breeze blowing gently upon his cheeks as he walked on the beach with his wife while his kids played in the sand. He imagined himself swinging on a hammock drinking diet soda with a funny umbrella in it. No meetings. No study. No hospital. No death. No meth addict.

In his daydream he could see out into the surf. The fish were teeming—just like the Bible said they should. Dolphins were jumping and flamingos were flapping. Without warning his daydream turned on him, like a lot of life, and breaking the water in the shallows of his imaginary island paradise was the beluga whale from the aquarium. The whale gave him that same stare of captivity.

"What was he doing here?" thought Butch. This is a tropical island and there are no belugas here!

"Go away! You're out of place."

He didn't actually say anything aloud because he was daydreaming. He was agitated though.

Snapping out of his thoughts he realized everyone else in the room was agitated. While he was away at the Island Paradise in his mind, a debate had sparked over the snacks for the event. The denomination had instructed that all due diligence be made to provide theme oriented snacks. This involved hours of work creating puffy pineapple treats, coconut balls made from almonds and mayonnaise, and something with celery, and a green jelled dessert which reminded Butch of antifreeze. Some in the group insisted that these denominationally sanctioned snacks be provided regardless of how much labor it took. On the other side were an equal number of folks who thought it was ridiculous. Cookies and punch were good enough for them when they were young, it would be good enough for the children who came.

Secretly, Butch figured the denomination must be getting some kind of kickback on the coconut balls or the food coloring manufacturers for promoting such treats. It sounded ridiculous, but one has to wonder who would come up with such things. Somewhere back in Nashville a Christianized Martha Stewart was diligently creating clever snacks with peanut butter, raisins, and pineapple.

A peacemaker had suggested the church be allowed to vote on it in a business meeting. Butch smiled thinking about how that discussion might go. He could hear it now, an hour of deliberation and then someone would make an impassioned plea that, "if we really loved Jesus we would do whatever it takes to provide coconut balls." The absurdity of it was overwhelming.

Butch spoke. "We are providing a ministry. We are not a restaurant or a bakery. We will provide whatever treats the congregation provides by their donations. The recipes for themed snacks will be put in the newsletter. To supplement these, we will also purchase cookies and punch at the grocery store. It would be a crime against the Holy Spirit to spend our time on frivolity while children may need our time, attention, hugs, and words of kindness. We must be more concerned

15

about affirming their worth and investing in their lives before they run out of time. I doubt they will care what kind of snacks we provide, especially if they haven't eaten in two days."

The two preschoolers in the backseat of that car were still on his mind.

Butch quickly collected his thoughts and gave the date for the next meeting and closed with a prayer.

It was 11:45. He still hadn't checked his email, worked through his physical inbox on his desk, made any phone calls, or even looked at next weeks worship service. All of these were things he intended to do before 10:30. He thought about trying to get something productive done, but all the talk about snacks made him hungry. He didn't even go back to his study. He placed his planner, papers, and the old stained daisy field coffee cup back on the hallway table and headed to his truck.

He was officially out to lunch.

The Noon Meal

Over the past few years lunch had become his favorite time of the day. He and his wife had bought a home just five minutes from the church building so he went home for lunch. With the kids at school it was a beautiful time when the two of them could talk, read through the mail together, or even play a game. His home was one of the few safe places he had. For Butch, safe meant he didn't have to worry about his words being taken out of context and quoted back to him in public. It also was freedom from the fear of having to suddenly transition from an administrator to a grief counselor. At home he could just be himself, and that was good.

Today his wife was not there. He had forgotten this until he got home, and it saddened him. She was knee deep in her own work. Some of the ladies of the congregation had invited her to a luncheon. It was a birthday party for one of the women retiring at the end of the month. Folks seemed to always include her in these things and she didn't mind because she liked the people. Butch, however, grumbled. Her spirituality was greater than his and he knew it.

He grumbled that it took her away from him, and he also grumbled that it was so expensive. She was constantly invited and expected to attend birthday parties, showers, and graduations. Along with these came gifts, cards, and gift bags. Some months they had spent as much as $300 just in gifts, not to mention the cost of all those luncheons at upper end restaurants.

Butch ate his bowl of cornflakes for lunch, pined for his wife and simmered his anger.

On this particular occasion she had bought a gift card for $30 to a bookstore for the gift, a $7 birthday card to put it in, and would have to buy lunch at a $20 a plate restaurant. The more he thought of this the angrier he became. The church had not given him more than a cost of living raise in five years. Colleagues of his got at least that and more pay, nice love offerings on their birthdays and Christmas, and they had less experience and education. On top of that, the church board only offered a very meager retirement plan. All this neglect in spite of the fact the church had done so well during his tenure.

The anger grew inside of him.

He grumbled to the dog about getting the shaft at Christmas.

Angrily he walked over to the kitchen counter. He wanted some juice. He snapped it out of the refrigerator, snapped off the lid and poured a glass. That is when he noticed it again.

Hanging on the coffee mug tree by the coffee pot was the cup he had bought at the aquarium with his wife and daughter. On the mug was that blasted beluga whale. The way the coffee mug dangled from its perch it almost floated surreally in the air. The flying beluga stared at him.

He felt as trapped as the whale must have felt. His church held him and his wife prisoner to their whims and desires. They were only better fed and well dressed versions of those two kids in the backseat of that car.

"We're all prisoners," he said to the dog. "We just have different cages."

Back to Work

By 1:00 P.M. he was back at the building and working at his study. He quickly moved through the stack of mail on his desk. Most all of it found an immediate home in the trash.

Invitation to a conference on church growth—trash.

A dynamic conference on emerging churches—trash.

17

Baby Boomer conference on worship—trash.

Gen X conference on ancient awareness—trash.

An opportunity to buy the new book, "Your Best Ministry Not Quite Now" by that TV preacher—trash.

He didn't open any of them. He did open the letter from the regional denominational office. It was a dour letter. The director was informing the churches of yet another quarter of sagging declines in giving. It was finally happening. The bank was breaking. Butch had noted it for years in board meeting after board meeting at the denominational headquarters that the methods were broken and someday the bank would be too. No one listened.

Now that the bank was breaking and future revenue could neither be projected nor promised suddenly talk was about reaching younger demographics.

But now it was too late.

No one believes Cassandra until the Trojan Horse is already inside the walls.

By contrast, his church was just fine. Their giving had increased, but then so had their intentional ministry toward younger families. They would never be a major player in church life, but they were steady, biblical, and committed to creating an authentic community. Butch had thought the issue through as part of his long range planning. He knew in his heart that the bureaucracy was really the only thing truly sick in American Christianity. It wasn't the local church. Some churches were sick and would die, but others would be used by God to take their place. God was at work, he just wasn't using man made towers of Babel which only exist to exercise power and control over local folks.

Butch didn't speak this often, and only behind closed doors. Telling the truth and saying what he really thought had gotten him in trouble a long time ago with the big wig church bosses. He would keep his mouth shut and do his job.

But today he felt like he was sick. Maybe there was something wrong with him. Perhaps a day off would be good. He needed to muster a cure of some sorts. He was tempted to lock up his study and leave. That, however, would be irresponsible. There was too much to do.

Once he cleared out all the mail he flipped around to his computer—

his trusted laptop. It was old and slow but familiar; like him. He had used this same laptop for almost seven years. Only his Greek New Testament was more used. His PC whizzed and clicked and he popped up the browser, logged in, and brought up his email.

Just like with the paper mail the email was a series of trash, click; trash, click; trash, click. It never ceased to amaze Butch how much spam he received. Lately he had been getting emails, "meet hot LDS singles in your area." He wondered just what kind of a Mormon would respond to that! It shamed him momentarily that the Mormons probably had higher morality than his brand. He whispered, "Kyrie Eleison." Somehow spam kept getting through about his need for a colon cleanse. Did his PC know something about his body he didn't? Probably not. Trash, click.

He had the music from the praise band emailed in for the second service. Good.

The music from the pianist was in for the first service. Good.

A reminder about a minister's luncheon on Thursday. He decided to go. He liked the Presbyterians.

Then there was an email from a military couple—he recognized the name. They had joined about two years ago when they were reassigned to the aircraft carrier. "I hope they are okay," he said to his computer.

Opening the email Butch read and began to cry. The sailor had been reassigned on the East Coast. They were leaving in two months, but they wouldn't be in church much because they were taking some time off to visit family in the Midwest and to find housing. Butch wept because he liked this man and his wife. Their children were a stabilizing presence in the children's department and they had contributed to the fellowship of the congregation.

Mainly he also wept because of the hurt and disconnect. Whenever a family left his church he felt the pain of separation. The best he could describe it was that it simply was a pastoral issue. When a relationship is made that is spiritual, breaking that relationship hurts.

He was happy for them because it was an advance in the sailor's career. But he was sad at the same time. Nonetheless this was a good separation.

The worse kind of separation was when he got the "Dear Pastor" letter that eventually ended with "we are leaving the church." This happened a lot in the first two or three years at the church but didn't happen much at all now. Yet about once or twice a year he would get one of those letters. It always felt the same. It felt like a sucker punch. He never saw it coming and it stung.

When people left the church he used to go try and talk them out of it. He didn't do that anymore. He realized people had all kinds of reasons why they leave a church and nothing he could say would change their mind.

Yet the pain was always there. Each time someone left he felt as if he had been fired from being their pastor. He felt he let them down. He felt he had not done something right. In talking to folks, though, he learned it was usually that a church down the street had a new gymnasium or a charismatic new song leader. Church has become like Wal-Mart and Costco. People shop for the best bargain in town. He had tried to think of a name for it. Maybe Godmart, or perhaps ChristCo. His wife called this marketing Stop-N-God, because for most church is only a matter of convenience.

He had been gazing at the email so long that his computer went to screen saver mode and began flashing pictures. The first picture it flashed was of his daughters playing in the mud last summer at Nana's house. The second picture was of their children swimming in the frigid waters of a lake in the upper Cascades. Their lips were blue. Butch chuckled at the memory. The third picture was of their trip last week to the aquarium. It was a snapshot he took behind glass. That beluga whale stared at him from the luminous screen.

The picture hovered on the screen in stasis for only the preprogrammed three seconds, but it felt like a millennia. In that millennia Butch felt a clamp close over his heart and begin to press. The tears welled up again and flowed. He cried at the captivity he was in. People kept coming and going in and out of his life like visitors to the zoo and there was nothing he could do to keep them there. He was trapped where he was while others could make whimsical choices.

"Oh, Lord," he prayed. "Help me be strong on this Monday. Why did I have to get this email on a Monday?" He cried a few more minutes and finally the eyes dried up. He cleared his head and nose. He swiveled and opened the bottom drawer of his desk. The very bottom drawer in which there was only one sheet of paper. Nothing else was allowed in that drawer.

He reached into the drawer and pulled out the paper. It was something he had written a decade ago. It had no date. It had no signature but he remembered exactly when he had written it. It was a Monday morning which felt just like this one. It was a letter he intended to never sign, but kept because he always felt like he wanted to.

He read through the letter again. He had read it many times, usually on Mondays.

Dear Church,

I can no longer function as your pastor. It is too hard. I can feel it making me bitter and I don't want to be this way. I have no more to give. I had hoped to spend the rest of my life living in community with you, but the demands are more than I can handle. I wish it would have worked out, but it hasn't. I am sure someone could do a better job anyway. You deserve better. Therefore I resign, effective immediately.

Butch Gregory

He might just sign it today. That whale was in his head. His own sermon was still preaching to him. The only way to get out of this captive life was to walk away from it and do something else. God never intended this kind of heartache. "I can have a better life than to live in this constant fear of growing bitter," he muttered.

He reached into his shirt pocket and pulled out his pen and clicked it. He prayed, "God I want to be faithful, but I also want to be free. Help me not do something stupid." There was a grand schizophrenic struggle taking place inside of him. He didn't really want to walk away, but he just couldn't take it anymore. He put the tip of the pen down to the paper and for the first time ever he pushed blue ink into the now yellowing piece of parchment.

"Butch, line one!" Mildred interrupted, yelling down the hallway and halting his pen. Her voice shattered the heavy air of decision like a baseball moving through a glass window.

Had the phone rung? He never heard it.

Because of that shoutus interruptus, a dot is as far as he got. He made no stroke. He looked again at the letter the way Eve must have

21

looked at the fruit. The way an addict looks at the junk. The way a sinner looks at temptation. His pen tempted him, for it was the key to his chains. He held relief in his right hand. He didn't have to answer line one. Freedom beckoned him. Shelter was just a stroke away.

Then he dropped it. He couldn't.

After taking a couple of calming deep breaths, he examined the blue ink dot. It ruined the pristine nature of his previously unsoiled resignation letter. His perception seemed to suddenly shift. The letter looked different to him now. It didn't look like a way out. It looked like a tragedy averted. It looked like a mistake.

Butch picked up the phone. Putting on his pastor voice he said, "This is Butch." He nodded his head as he listened to the other end. "I'm on my way. I'll be there in about twenty minutes." He paused for just a moment, listening and then added, "I love you too." Butch hung up, reached into his top drawer, grabbed his pocket ministry Bible and headed out the door. He walked past Mildred's desk and said without stopping to make eye contact, "I'm on my way to the hospital."

The Hospital

The phone call was from Laura Singleton. She called to tell him that her husband, Bob, was in the emergency room at county hospital. In the past two years Bob had two heart episodes, one a full blown heart attack. There was talk of a bypass, but because of his age and increasing weakness from his other procedures they decided to leave it alone. His health had declined rapidly in the last month. It had been a while since they were even able to be at worship services. Both Bob and Laura knew it was near the end. Butch had hoped it wouldn't be this soon.

The Singletons were an older couple who had been in the church for decades. Butch had renewed their vows at their sixtieth wedding anniversary. He had baptized their grandchildren. He had eaten at their table.

Two weeks earlier Butch had come out to their house and had communion with the two of them in their home. Bob couldn't really swallow anything as hard as a Protestant communion wafer so Butch and the deacon with him ground the wafer into pieces, mixed it with a little of the juice from the cup, blessed it, and placed it on his lips. Just like Jesus was broken to pieces so many years ago, so too was it in the Singleton living room.

It was a holy moment, that Thursday afternoon. Bob had cried. Butch cried. The deacon cried. Laura cried. Butch had ended the communion service by repeating the sentiment of Christ's words saying, "Jesus will not drink of this cup until he drinks it with us in heaven." Now on the drive over to the hospital Butch wondered if today would be the day Jesus and Bob shared that drink.

Butch cried on his way to the hospital. This was turning out to be a tougher than usual Monday. He also realized why he could never sign that letter in his drawer. God had called him to do this. He loved Bob and Laura. He wanted to be driving to see them in their moment of need.

He arrived at the hospital and made his way to the ER. The woman at the desk recognized him and smiled. "Hello, Father," she said. Butch had seen this same woman for years at the front desk.

He replied, "Can Bob Singleton have a brief visitor?"

"I'll go check, Father."

The woman was obviously religious enough to know that he was in ministry but not in tune enough to know he wasn't Roman Catholic. Earlier in his ministry this would have bothered him and he would have corrected her. It didn't anymore, and he wouldn't dare.

As he waited he thought about the conference he attended earlier that year down in Portland. The speaker had talked about how the church of the future wouldn't do hospital ministry. He had cited that all the key leadership gurus of the day were encouraging pastors and ministers to spend their time leading like CEO's and not doing pastoral ministries. Butch understood the impetus behind it and had taken the time to train lay men and women to do pastoral care. Yet, he could never envision a world in which people who were called into the gospel ministry didn't bring comfort and the awareness of Christ's presence into the scariest moments of people's lives. Jesus would never say, "I'm too busy to go to the hospital."

The duty nurse came back out through the big electronically operated double doors and said, "Father, Mr. Singleton is in stall seven. You can stay a few minutes."

"Thank you," he said, and added, "Blessings."

23

Walking through the ER's triage and its lack of privacy he saw what looked like a car accident in stall three, one child in a makeshift cast in stall five, and a couple of older folks attached to cords coming out of machines monitoring vital signs like heart rate and respiration in stalls six and nine.

He suddenly caught Laura's face through a crack in the curtain which had blocked off stall seven. Their daughter was also standing beside Bob's bed. He cursed his memory. He couldn't remember the daughter's name. Sally. Sue. Sonia. Susie. Shonda. Shelly. S S S S S Stacey. That's it. Stacey. He said a silent and quick prayer, "Thank you Jesus."

Sneaking behind the curtain he gave Laura a big hug and gave her daughter a sideways hug and said, 'It's good to see you Stacey." Stacey was like many baby-boomer children. She walked away from the faith of her builder parents. He had once tried to talk to her about Jesus, God and church but she informed him she did not believe in organized religion. He tried to assure her there was nothing organized about his church. She didn't get the joke and things kind of fell apart from there. He only saw her on Mother's Day, Easter, and Christmas Eve.

And now at the hospital.

Butch quickly turned his attention to Bob. He looked fine, but a little pale and very frightened. He was hooked up to all kinds of wires. Butch assumed these were heart monitors. He carefully and gently hugged Bob.

Butch looked around for a place to sit but the room was cramped and crowded with the three of them standing there. Butch had learned hospitals are never designed thinking about the needs of people who might be with the sick. In fact, he didn't think people designed anything in hospitals thinking about the needs of the sick. Everything was built for the doctors and nurses.

"I hear you're not feeling well, Bob," said Butch, stating the obvious.

"No, I'm not," Bob replied. "I think this might be the end. My chest hurt. It felt like a truck parked on me. I blacked out. Laura called 911."

"We're praying for you to get better." The phrase sounded so weak coming out of his mouth. Butch believed in prayer but he wished there were more. He wished he was like the apostles in the Bible who would raise people up and tell them to take up their mat and go.

"I will get better preacher," Bob said with a very low breath. It was all the energy he could get to talk and his voice was very low. Butch had to lean in to hear him speak. "I will get better because I think I'm almost gone to heaven."

Butch knew the words were true. Down deep, he just knew. So, Butch did his job. He put aside for a moment his emotions and remembered that his primary responsibility was to prepare souls for the transition from this world to the next. To do this he knew he had to be a non-anxious presence in the room. That was the way an old seminary professor had put it. That task had seemed so simple in the classroom. In times like this it seemed impossible.

Screwing his spiritual courage to the sticking place, Butch took Bob's hand, looked him in the eyes and said, "Bob, that may not be true. But in case it is, are you ready? Are you at peace with God? Is there anything we need to talk about?"

In Butch's experience about ninety percent of the time the person would say no, but then immediately start to talk about something from the past which needed processing. Surprisingly, though, Bob took his other hand, put it over Butch's hand in such a way that he had a double grip and said, "Preacher, I am ready to meet Jesus. I am only worried about my wife. I will miss her and I worry about her."

Butch told him, "The Lord will take care of his flock, Bob. Your wife belonged to Christ before she ever belonged to you. He will continue to nurture her and care for her until at last, you will be reunited in heaven."

At that, Butch read a brief passage from the Gospel of John and then took Laura's hand, asked Stacey to take her mother's hand, and even asked the nurse who had been coming in and out if she wanted to join in, but she declined. He touched Bob's forehead and prayed the old familiar Psalm:

> *"Lord, you are our shepherd. We shall not be in want. You have made us to lie down in green pastures. You lead us beside still waters. You have restored our soul. You have guided Bob in paths of righteousness for your namesake. Even though he, and we, walk through the valley of the shadow of death, none of us will fear evil. For we know that by the power of the Holy*

Spirit you are with us. Your rod, and your staff—they comfort us. You have prepared a table before us in the presence of our great ancient enemy, the enemy of death. You anoint our heads with oil. Our cup of blessing has run over. Surely goodness and love will follow Bob, Laura, and their entire family, all the days of our lives. And we will dwell in the house of the Lord forever. Amen."

After some small talk with the family, Butch made his way out of the stall and down the hallway. He leaned into the front desk and said, "Thank you" to the woman who had greeted him.

"Have a nice day Father," she replied.

"I will."

He picked up his cell phone and dialed his wife before he even got out of the parking garage. He asked her if she could pick up their oldest daughter. He usually picked her up on his way home from work in the afternoons. But he was so far behind. She asked if everything was okay and he said sure.

He lied, and he knew it. Was that a sin of omission?

He didn't want to tell her about Bob or the email about the family being reassigned on the East Coast. His wife liked them all and the news would be a big blow to her. He would tell her tonight. No sense ruining her afternoon. He just told her he was running way behind.

That, however, was a very true statement.

On the drive back he was thinking about all the things he still needed to do. He was yet to look at his sermon for next week. He hated to get behind on that. He would pick up his folder and a couple of books to take home and work on it tonight after dinner in his home study. His best sermons were written there anyway. It was the only place he could work undisturbed.

He also had yet to return any phone calls. He knew there would be several of those. Then there was the family that visited yesterday. He wanted to follow up with them and he needed to plan that new outreach ministry to twenty somethings. There was something else he needed to do today, but he couldn't remember what it was.

He was working very hard at what that thing he couldn't remember was as he drove. He was going along at a good clip and passed by a Transit Bus. On the side of the bus was a giant billboard moving at

26

thirty miles an hour. Butch could hardly believe what he saw. On the billboard was a promo for the aquarium and there was that beluga whale again. It stared right at him, again.

Butch's face flushed and he began to sweat.

"Why is this whale stalking me?" he shouted to the dashboard. Nervously, with both hands firmly on the steering wheel he snuck another peek at the moving billboard. As he did, the whale winked at him.

Butch swerved and almost hit a Toyota hybrid before regaining control of his SUV. The bus sped away and he pulled over on the side of the road. He counted to ten. He controlled his breathing. He said a prayer. "Lord, please tell me what you're trying to tell me. Am I going crazy?" He listened for a response.

Nothing.

He waited a few more minutes.

Still no response.

"Maybe I am going crazy."

Pulling back onto the road Butch made a mental note to take next Monday off. Maybe he would take the rest of this week off.

He got back to his study at about 4:15 P.M. He rifled through five phone messages that came in while he was away. Mildred had gone. Brian had gone. No one else was there. The janitor would come in at 5:30 and the Twelve Steps group would be here at 6:00. He tidied up his desk, taking care to put the unsigned but despoiled resignation letter back in its own private drawer.

He returned the phone calls. One was to the maintenance chairperson about repairing the lights broken by vandals. Two were to other pastors in the area about the ministers' luncheon this week. A fourth was another benevolence request. Someone had gotten $1,300 behind on his power bill. He forwarded the benevolence to his deacon officer. The last one was a couple wanting marriage counseling. He returned the call and left a voice mail. He powered down his PC which had been running all afternoon but unused.

He shoved it into his satchel along with his sermon notepad and a couple of books he had grabbed to look through tonight. He would preach this Sunday on forgiveness. Particularly he wanted to talk about how we must learn to forgive ourselves for our past. He might reference that famous passage, "God knows our frailties that we are but dust." He would work on that at home and he would also write his Monday blog. He also had a book to finish reading tonight.

At 5:13 he left, turned off the light and went home. On the way out of the door he spied his coffee cup on the hallway table. He almost went back inside to put it in the kitchen or to put in his study. But he was just too tired. He would get it in the morning.

Home

As soon as he walked in the door he smelled the savory supper his wife was cooking. The aroma wooed him into the kitchen, where he heard his children chatting with their mother. He kissed his wife and grabbed a diet soda, and talked to his family. They talked about band, the school play, and that bratty boy on the softball team. His wife told him all about the luncheon and how she enjoyed it. He felt a little guilty for his pity party at lunchtime. He didn't tell his wife anything about it, though. He asked when supper would be ready and she said in about forty-five minutes.

He walked into the living room and plopped onto his recliner. He wanted to rest a moment. Flipping on the television he found his favorite station—the Discovery Channel. There was some program on about climate change or something but Butch didn't care. He just wanted to power down, like he had powered down his computer.

He felt himself dozing off to sleep. His last thought before drifting into the nether regions of the brain was that his wife would wake him when supper was ready.

In slumber he found no solace. The menace which had haunted him all day was waiting there for him behind his eyelids. Butch dreamed of the whale. The beluga whale was white like finely carved ivory. She was big, many times bigger than the beluga at the aquarium. Butch was looking at the whale from the pole of an 18th century sailing vessel with riggings and tackle all around. But in the dream the perch was not a rounded lookout. It was a giant pulpit and Butch was wearing the ancient clerical robes ministers wore 300 years ago. In his right hand was his preaching Bible, and in his left hand was his coffee cup. The cup was running over.

In a flash, the way things do in dreams, Butch's elevated lookout pulpit lunged off the boat and hovered right over the giant beluga whale. The whale looked at Butch and shook her head in a disapproving manner. Then the whale spoke.

"You've had a tough day, my friend. All day I've tried to warn you, but you wouldn't listen. Now hear me." The whale's voice was deep and soothing; but also frighteningly dominant. It was a unique sounding voice Butch had never quite heard before.

Butch protested the whale's opinion of the day events. "What do you mean you were trying to warn me? You were my biggest problem. You haunted me and tormented me. You almost caused me to have an accident on the road. Are you trying to kill me? Is that it? Go ahead! I've had enough of this sad world anyway. It doesn't make any sense to me anyway."

The whale smiled, like the Cheshire cat and said, "Problem? You think I'm the problem? The problem is you, preacher. You are on the verge of giving into despair. Despair is not a good place to be. You fret about things beyond your reach as if you were God. You are angry, and you have no right to be.

"Do you not remember that God loves the world more than you love the world? Do you not remember that he loves the children in the backseat of that car more than you? Do you not remember that he is aware of how hardheaded his people can be? Do you not remember that God has been ushering dying people from this life into the next since time began?

"Do you not remember that God has chosen to use you to be a part of his expression of love? How can you do that if you give up? How can you do that if you give into despair? How can you serve God when you serve your own self pity? When the Lord called you to ministry he told you it would be hard and that the people would not be easy. You knew that when you signed up. Are you surprised that it is tough? Are you surprised there are sacrifices? Do you not remember how comfortable your life is compared to so many around the world and across time whose title of pastor meant death and torture?"

There was a good long pause. Butch said nothing.

Suddenly the whale erupted deep and loud saying, "Well, do you. Answer me, I demand an answer."

"Well, no, I guess not since you put it that way," Butch said meekly.

"Where were you," the whale said in a strong, vibrating tone, "when the Lord gave birth to the church? Tell me if you are so old and wise. Where were you, when the Lord defeated death and Hell forever? Tell me if you are so strong? Where were you, when the Lord brought Bob and Laura Singleton into the Kingdom of God, into the family of faith? Tell me, if you are so important? Where were you, when the Lord made humanity in his image? Tell me, if you are so wise as to advise God on what to do? Speak, I demand an answer."

Butch stood on his dreamy pulpit with is head down and said, "I have nothing to say."

The whale responded, "Good. I'm glad we got that straight. It will never be easy, Butch, to do the Lord's work. They kill prophets and pastors. But he is always with you."

With a jerk Butch awoke to the smell of cheese steak and fries. His wife called out to him, "Honey, for the third time, dinner's ready!" Out of reflex Butch stood and looked over at the TV. It was still on the same program, and swimming on the frigid blue waters in high definition were beluga whales frolicking in the freedom of their native habitat; right where God wanted them. To most of the species on God's good earth, the ice chunks and frozen environment would be devastating. But to the whales it was home. They thrived in the inhospitable climate.

So too must he thrive among the frigid icebergs of ministry.

Then his phone rang. He answered it. It was a short conversation and he said a few words. He walked into the kitchen, grabbed his keys and told his wife he would be back in about an hour.

"Where are you going? Dinner just got ready!" She seemed more than a little miffed as she said this.

He gave a sad smile and said, "Laura Singleton just called. Bob died about fifteen minutes ago."

Convocation

(This story won 3rd prize in the 2009 ACM Christian Writing Contest)

All worshipers of images are put to shame,
who make their boast in worthless idols;
worship him, all you gods!—Psalm 97:7

The meeting place smelled of sweet smoke. An aroma of cedar and myrrh was strong, but pleasant. It was noticeable enough to get the nose's attention but not so strong that it elicited a cough or throat clearing. The scent wafted high through to the top of the large chamber.

The room was lit from above with dazzling torches mounted on large Doric columns. At the top of each column was an impressive golden capital covered with elegant engravings of plants and vines, lilies and flowers. The columns rose to seventy feet, but there was no roof. The hall was open aired. A row of six titanic columns equidistant apart lined each side of the room framing it in a perfect square. Fifteen feet behind the columns lay a stone wall that stretched immeasurably upward beyond the columns. These walls seemed to elevate for miles. The moon hung overhead with Venus nearby marking the night sky.

In the middle of the room was a large stone altar made from rugged rock. This stone had never been chiseled by hands. The five craftsmen who formed it were named Time, Wind, Rain, Heat, and Cold. Neither iron tool nor hammer had ever touched this megalith. The top and the sides of the stone altar were stained with blood; human blood.

"This reminds me of Athens, or maybe Thebes," said Zeus—to no one in particular. "Yes. I indeed like the columns. Oh look, hanging there in the night sky, why yes it is, lovely Aphrodite's namesake. This room is almost perfect. It is worthy of Noble Hector or my strong son Hercules."

"It reminds me more of Memphis!" barked another voice. The voice was irritated and annoyed; like one who was spoiling for a fight, or at least a good argument.

Zeus responded bitterly as he snarled his upper lip, "I thought I smelled the foul stench of Egypt. Greetings, Ra."

"Why have you called me here, O Zeus the Indulgent?"

"Me?" said Zeus inquisitively. "I was about to ask you the same thing."

Seconds later two more figures appeared around the stone altar. It was a couple: male and female. Both had cone shaped heads and elongated faces.

"Who are you?" asked Zeus.

"I am Baal, Lord of the Sky. This is my consort Asherah. Now who, pray tell, are you?"

"I am Zeus Almighty, King of Olympus, Son of Kronos and god of the Hellenes." Zeus raised his hands and shot a dazzling array of lightening bolts into the upper reaches of the chamber.

"And I am Ra—Dread Lord of the Under…"

"We know who you are. I could spot your stench anywhere." Asherah cut him off indignantly.

Within seconds the room became populated with all manner of figures: the many armed Shiva, Marduk, the Buddha, Tao, Thor, Sky-Spirit, the feather serpent Quetzalcoatl, along with many, many others. There were thousands of deities who suddenly appeared. Some were animals like the Native American Wolf or the Hindu Brahma. Some were more personified symbols or images, like the Tao or Humanism. After a brief hubbub they all stopped asking why they were there and, curiously, began to mingle like people would at a cocktail party.

The deities seemed to form in affinity groups. Those from the Mediterranean Basin grouped together, and those from the East stood together, the ancient Celtic and Norse deities from Europe mingled as best warrior gods can in a social context, and the mystical tribal gods from the American continents fused into something of a homogenous group. Allah, however, stood off alone in a corner and fumed while plotting domination. He was searching for a burkha to put over the ancient fertility goddess. This particular goddess is known by many names, the most common one is Isis.

Some were having fun with the event. Zeus was taking bets on exactly how long it would take the Sumerian Moon goddess Ishtar to seduce the chaste Buddha. Others were academically comparing and contrasting aspects of their cult. They discussed such things as requirements for novitiates, priestly adherence, ceremonial actions, and holy texts. It was a grand dialogue of comparative religion at the penultimate perspective. That was, until the main event began.

Just when everyone was getting comfortable and had forgotten where they were and the mysterious circumstances of their gathering; a light.

A great light shown and filled the chamber.

The light was pure. The light was penetrating. Oden held out his hand and the light made an X-Ray of his digits. In a moment of panic Zeus again shot out lightening bolts from his hands, but these seemed pale and yellow compared to the perfect light. The light started with a glow and slowly built up in intensity. When it reached an unbelievable zenith of photoscopic power a billion decibel choir rang out, seemingly from nowhere but everywhere, "Alleluia!" Then, just as suddenly, the light flashed out.

A man stood in its place. He was standing on the blood stained rock altar. At his appearance all the deities were pushed—not pulled—pushed by the force of the man's gravity toward the marble floor. The gravitational force of the push flattened them prostrate onto their stomachs with their face down. Proud Ra fought to stay on his knees but he could not resist the intractable pressure pushing him into a fully humiliating position.

The man on the stone altar smiled.

"You may rise," he said to the pantheon.

Shiva popped up and proudly asked, "Who do you think you are?" With the question he pointed all of his flailing hands at the man standing on the stone. To the question, the man replied, "I am." As the word "am" came out of his mouth, the push from above forced all the deities onto the ground once more.

The one on the bloody altar, the only one left standing, sat down upon the stone. It now no longer looked like a stone altar. It now looked like a throne. In his right hand was an iron rod. In his left hand was a shepherd's crook. His legs and feet were bronze. He wore a simple white tunic.

He lifted his iron rod and regally proclaimed, "You may stand. But no more questions."

They all slowly came to their full height. No one said a word, but many glances were exchanged. The dominant feeling among the convocation was confusion and fear. Never before had these deities been so powerless. A moment or two passed and the seated one began to speak.

"My name is Jesus, the Alpha and the Omega."

The god of war Ares shouted, "How can that be? We killed you on that hillside. I remember it. I was there with my soldiers."

Hades chimed in, "Yeah, I was there too. You died. Why won't you stay dead? You're breaking all the rules." The other deities chimed in with similar affirmations, "I was there when we crucified you. I remember!"

Jesus just smiled. "Obviously you are not as powerful as you thought. I am resurrection and I am life. But now it is time for judgment upon all the gods. Let me begin with the greatest pretender of all, Zeus."

Instantly Zeus was front and center before the throne. He opened his mouth to make an argument, a defense, or even a plea. Yet nothing came out. For the first time in his existence Zeus was silent.

"You are not allowed to speak. You have spoken too much already; O Thundering Zeus of the Hellenes. You are guilty. You are indeed guilty of being a bad example. You have reflected all that is evil in people: Power, lust, capricious whims, vengeful spite, and anger. You have no love, only eros. You have no compassion, only pathos. You are a sham. You are a bully. You and the whole pantheon over which you preside are evil."

The chief god of the Hellenes knew it was true. He cringed. There was nothing noble in him. Suddenly and without warning Zeus was moved out and another stood in his place. Actually, it was two others who stood before the altar-throne. The Semitic gods Baal and Asherah of Palestine stood where Zeus had just been.

"Baal, you are not alone in your wickedness. Asherah and her evil poles have done more harm than Zeus could ever hope to. No one really ever believed in him. Yet you, you have time and time again lead the peoples of the Near East away from their journey to true faith. You have lured them in with prosperity and wealth, good harvests and fine climate. None of which, incidentally, you have any control over. The only work you ever did was to lie and take credit for what I created.

"Under every green tree and on every hilltop in Palestine you deceived people, male and female. In this deception you model the old liar, Hasatan, and led my people astray. You have added sexual iniquity, prostitution, and violence to humanity. You stand condemned

35

as did your prized acolyte, Jezebel."

Within the next few minutes Jesus moved very quickly through many of the shuddering deities. Ra was deemed demonic and oppressive. The pyramids of Egypt do not celebrate his greatness, but stand as a monument to his own vanity. The eagles of the Native American folk religion were dismissed as being too distance, uncaring, and impersonal. Christ condemned Thor as a cheap imitation of Zeus and with the added guilt of encouraging the heinous terrorism of piracy. Quickly the pace intensified as the God of gods summarily judged one false deity after another.

Then the pace slowed down again as the major world deities came before the stone throne.

"Shiva—I will allow you to represent all of the Hindu gods. You have held billions of people hostages to a caste system which benefits the wealthy and protects the privileged. Have you no shame? Do you not see the potential beauty in releasing people from their cultural shackles? You invent oppression and call it religion. I call it what it is, pure evil!

"You have added to your evil the belief system of past lives and future incarnations. What nonsensical bilge! Do you not know that man is noble? Each human being—woman, man or child is as unique as the Milky Way or as vast as the depth of the oceans? You and your ilk have missed the mark terribly in your estimation of what exactly comprises humanity."

The Lord moved on.

"Oh Buddha, he who is not a god yet venerated; not divine but the enlightened one. Truly, truly I say unto you, you were not far from authentic revelation. In you I find no violence or greed. But you have likewise missed the concept.

The secret to enlightenment is not within the individual. No amount of reflection or meditation can bring truth. It only brings the hint of truth. True enlightenment emanates from the outside and penetrates the soul. You reversed the order and put humanity as the source of spiritual knowledge. What a terrible usurpation. Yes, you were close but still so far away. In your nearness you did not recognize the distance still to go. Instead you mistook *almost there* as *arrived*. This misjudgment led to arrogance and certainty."

A tear formed in the fat Buddha's eye for he knew the truth.

"The Tao must now be examined. Tao, you reflect the timeless truths which I have placed in the created order. There is indeed a balance in nature. Hot must have cold, day must have night, summer is tempered by winter, male is only complete with female. Humans have a yin for every yang and a yang for every yen. Opposites do attract.

"Nevertheless, you are a fraud. You claim to be the way when there can only be one way. I am. There is nothing in you which brings the harmony you preach. Description is your only gift."

There was only one more left. All had been exposed as insufficient and deceptive. All had been judged, except one. Jesus, still sitting upon the throne called him by name. "Allah," he shouted. "Come here.

"Your time has come. I saved you for the end. You are more recent than these ancient false religions. As with all the others there are elements of truth in some of your words. There is only one God. Alms are proper. Fasts are good. Hospitality pleases me. Good works are a blessing.

"But you have led the sons of Ishmael astray taking them down the path of violence. For centuries you have conquered with the sword, the machine gun, and the suicide bomber. You use fear as a spiritual tactic. You have oppressed the daughters of Eve. You are guilty of turning human beings into automatons. You have rejected your heritage of learning and science. You are guilty of abusing the human race which I made in my image. Therefore, you are guilty of abusing and therefore blaspheming me."

The truth of what the Lord had said to all of these deities penetrated the hard hearts of all. They knew their place in the cosmos. They were not what they thought they were. They stood before him shamed.

King Jesus began to speak to the group as a whole now. "You are created in the image of man; gods and goddesses he made you in his own likeness. Male and female he made you. From his imagination he formed you; out of his own futile thinking he molded you and gave you substance. You were created by him and he breathed into you his own sexual appetites, violent tendencies, legalism, and desire for undisciplined spirituality without moral absolutes in order to justify his sin."

As these words were spoken each of the deities stood with

outstretched arms and said in one voice, repeating over and over again:

Holy, holy, holy is the Lord God Almighty,
Who was and is and is to come
Worthy are you, our Lord and God,
To receive glory and honor and power,
For you created all things,
And by your will they existed and were created.

The brilliant light re-appeared and grew in ever more intensity. As it came to a crescendo the repeated spoken words were louder and louder until the blend of sound and light were one unified sensory experience. It was as if they were in the exploding core of a supernova. Then it flashed out and became silent. All the deities slowly dissolved into nothingness. Only Jesus was left.

He sighed deeply, stood up, and said, "Now it is time for judgment to begin with the household of God."

My Olympic Mountains

The sun settles in behind the mountains, the Olympic mountains.
　No wonder the ancients thought the
　gods
　　　lived upon the lofty peaks; what
　　　more beautiful place on earth could there be
　　　which gods might attend the symphonic
　　　sunset. Blue blends into orange, orange
　　　erupts into yellow and it is all surrounded
　　　by pink.

It doesn't require a lot of imagination to put an old man Zeus
　atop
　　　the beautiful mountain, partaking of
　　　ambrosia, or of Hera or even some peasant
　　　girl he picked up. Kronos hesitates over the speckles of
　　　winters waning snowcap and stands still while
　　　the fates await the next movement
　　　of beauty.

But the sun has set on the great Olympian gods of
　lore:
　　　Athena, Hermes, Artemis and Hephaestus
　　　have taken their place upon the pile of
　　　characters in stories, for they were as
　　　false and fleeting as the shadows cast on the rock
　　　crags on the mountain as the sun passed
　　　overhead.

In a reversal, new titans emerged not too long ago, the would-be gods upon
the mountain
　　　named Reason, a snooty god who commands legions
　　　of adherents who do congregate on university
　　　campuses. Do not forget measured Science, god
　　　of explanation with adepts that speak an unknown tongue
　　　where verbs and nouns become charts. Then Self, the god in the
　　　mirror.

These gods evolved out of the gray matter goo of the brains own
ego
making Reason, who doubted all but itself. Then
Science took shape and tried to kill faith
in everything but Reason. They formed a duality
as sovereign monarchs. Behold, now Self topples
her/his progenitors; it is neither rational nor is measurable. It only
consumes.

Trouble with being king of the mountain is staying on top. Competing deities
must be wary
for siege war craft pile against such as Zeus,
The Buddha, or Darwin; all of whom tumble hard
and usually quite hard. They leave behind
no followers but many marble temples and telescopes
or all kinds of beautiful relics curiously called
art-i-facts.

On the mountain are beautiful feet which bring euangelion;
for the real king, the one not imagined there yet who imagined it there,
refuses to yield.
He is the everlasting one who has revealed himself from mountain
to mountain: Mt. Moriah to Mt. Zion to Mt. Calvary to the lowly
seven hills of Rome. Through mountains tall and small he alone
is the king who holds the sun perched over my Olympic
Mountains.

Ekklesia Awry

Father, please forgive me.
I didn't know. I didn't know I got it all wrong.
Yet all of the books I am reading these days,
keeping singing the same old song.

It's hard to grasp.
Emergent seeker purpose and simple
all form a scary church code.
But I want the easy path walking up to the Temple.

It is too much.
Church should be a people and place
where folks can go with their fragile spirit,
And find not-so-common grace.

Christ, this is hard.
There is no shortage of blow hard published people
with advice acronyms charts and plans.
Why do I really want to hang them from a steeple?

Where did it change?
When did worship and praise fall to the fad?
Is anyone else wringing their hands,
thinking it can't all be that bad?

Maybe in a cloister
I could find a quiet place to hide.
There I would ride the third-wave out
while the bride of Christ commits church-i-cide.

Spirit, this isn't right.
Has it been this wrong for two millennia?
Did Wesley Luther Bede Augustine and Athanasius
all contribute to church dementia?

Help me, I'm drowning.
Not like Peter on the water.
Instead in a sea of lofty words and schema;
and boiling too, the rhetoric gets hotter.

And can it be?
That Jesus will wait to come back
until the jot and tittle of every bad idea
will get a whirl around the track?

Sell Out

"We can cut, or we can beg. Those are our options."

The middle aged pastor knew it was true. For the last twenty minutes he and fourteen other people had listened to one report after another of financial woes for Old First Church. It had not been a good meeting and he feared it was only going to get worse. The Chairman of the Board repeated the same phrase, "We can cut, or we can beg for more money from the members. Those are our options."

Giving trends were down. That was the first report they had received. Membership wasn't down, just giving. Fewer families were tithing. Most people gave, but only about thirty percent of the families tithed. The average giving percentage was two percent per family. A couple of board members mumbled about creeping materialism in the modern age but the pastor knew something no one else did. Only three of the board members tithed. Paradoxically, none of the three who tithed were the ones complaining about materialism.

At the same time giving was down, expenses were up. That was the second bit of bad news. Health insurance premiums for the staff were skyrocketing, everyone expected that but it was the other things that shocked the board. Utilities had almost doubled. They decided to stop heating the building for evening activities to cut back on some expenses and to put keyed boxes around all thermostats. They suspected the quilting auxiliary ladies kept turning up the heat, and that had to be stopped.

"Maybe they could quilt some scarves for themselves," someone had quipped.

In addition to utilities, the denomination was putting pressure for more money to be sent to the regional office. Pastor explained that the regional branch had increased expenditures and fewer churches were sending their usual amount. Even as he said the words, he realized the denomination was undergoing the same thing Old First Church was at a local level.

On top of all of this, the third report the board heard was that the building program was on hold because they were out of money. No new donations were coming in, and they had only gotten architect drawings. The cost of an architect was far more than they thought it would be.

Pastor worried the project might be put off, and that would be bad. The Methodists had just built a new multi-million dollar gymnasium and he knew if he didn't at least match it, he would lose some of his families who really wanted a church that had a gymnasium. Their new plans included a swimming pool as a 'one up' on the Presbyterians. He could count ten families he knew he would lose if they didn't build, because he had stolen them from the Baptists when they built the youth building two years ago.

But that was when money was good.

Now, it wasn't so good. The economy had tanked. Many people in his church were unemployed or under-employed. The food pantry ministry was continually having to be restocked from overuse. The church was simply in a financial crunch. It was obligated to spend more than it was taking in; and unlike the government, churches are not allowed to print money.

The question was still on the table. Would the church board vote to cut or plead for more money? Pastor opened his mouth to speak, "Well, cutting makes sense, but I don't think we can cut enough to make up for these shortfalls unless we cut staff. I don't want to do that. I also think we could plead for more money, but honestly, does anyone think it will work? Most of our people are up to their eyeballs in debt and are facing difficult choices with their own pocketbook. Let's take a week to pray about it and also to work through and see if we're missing something. What we really need is new revenue streams, but I don't know where to get them."

It wasn't a very good pep talk, but it was all he could come up with. He prayed and dismissed them.

When Pastor arrived at his study the next morning the financial doldrums were still on his mind, but he tried to push it aside. He did typical Wednesday stuff: a little writing, newsletter oversight, some reading, and email. Around 11:00 A.M. he returned phone calls. One of them was Harry. Harry was on his board and had been at the meeting last night, but hadn't said anything. Harry had called at 8:05 that morning. Pastor was worried something was wrong.

He punched up the number on his Blackberry, "Hey Harry, it's Pastor."

"Hi Pastor," Harry replied in a deep confident voice. "Can I take you to lunch at the country club today?"

"Sure, I'll save my tuna fish sandwich for another day. But, Harry, is everything okay?"

Harry paused. "Yeah, everything is good. It might even be getting better. There is just something I need to run by you. Look, though, I've gotta run. I have a meeting with my boss in five minutes. I'll see you at noon."

"Yes, I'll be there."

As he hit the *end call* he worried that Harry was leaving the church. This is usually how that went. In the last decade he had had seven 'we're leaving the church' lunches at that blasted country club. He assumed Harry would be switching to the Methodists now that he knew the gym and swimming pool wouldn't happen.

At lunch they made small talk and as the food came Harry looked at Pastor and said, "I think I may have your new revenue stream."

"Really?"

"Yes, but you may not like it. Pastor, you know I work for the Coca-Cola company and we're aggressively looking for new markets."

"I know," said Pastor. "But we already have five Coke machines at the church. I do not know if we need another one."

Harry giggled, "I'm not talking about pop machines, Pastor. I'm talking about sponsorship. Next month is our big Labor Day Picnic. I cleared it with my regional marketing manager this morning, we will pay the church a nice sum of money to sponsor the picnic."

"You want to sponsor a church picnic?" Pastor was more than a little confused. "Whoever heard of that? I mean, that sounds crazy."

"We do it all the time," Harry began, "Usually for civic organizations or big regional events. You wouldn't have to do anything and it would not affect the ministry base at all. You know Carolyn and I have been at the church for years. We want to do the right thing, and would not let it become a problem. We'd just make a couple of signs that say COCA COLA PRESENTS THE ANNUAL OLD FIRST CHURCH LABOR DAY PICNIC. We would also want to set a couple of vendors to sell soda and candy and maybe some hot dogs. In exchange for that, we'd give the church a big hunk of change."

"That does sound easy," Pastor stumbled in his speech, "but, what's in it for Coke? Why would they do this?"

"Well," he explained, "for starters there are about a thousand people who usually come out from the church. That is a pretty good marketing sample. Second, you hold the event in the park all day in the middle of summer. We estimate as many as 10,000 people might see our banner or purchase from our vendors. Because we sponsor you, we will impact more than just people there for the picnic. It's all about branding and name recognition. Coca-Cola didn't get to be the most recognized item in the world by accident. We know what we are doing."

Pastor still looked a little skeptical. Harry continued, "Old First Church is a well known and established congregation and when people think about how much they love you, we want them to think of Coca Cola too. It is a simple matter of our needs converging with your needs in the ever changing matrix of point of contact marketing. Its synergy."

It all made sense, sort of. Pastor scratched his head and thought for a moment.

"I'll have to take it to the board."

"Understood," said Harry. "I'll have contracts drawn up for the board to look at next Tuesday night when we meet."

When the board met the following week, it surprised Pastor exactly how easily they adapted to the idea. No one objected. No one said anything negative at all. The board was happy for the "partnership agreement." That is what the paperwork called it. Pastor couldn't help but wonder exactly what they were partnering to do? Were they now selling soda, or was Coke now offering salvation?

As the day of the picnic approached, he expected some complaints. He had already brainstormed with his wife as to who would complain. The Women's Auxiliary most certainly would protest. There were some families in the church who were a little more socially conservative than the rest of the congregation. These families tended to home-school and listen to talk radio. He expected them to protest. He also knew the emeritus pastor from the 1970's and 80's would protest. He knew it was coming.

Nevertheless, he put on his Hawaiian shirt, sunglasses, and sunscreen and courageously screwed his courage to the sticking point and headed out for the COCA COLA PRESENTS THE ANNUAL OLD FIRST CHURCH LABOR DAY PICNIC. It took almost as long to say as it did to drive there.

For the most part the picnic was the usual affair. Food, drinks, games, some loud band music, and churchy talk from people sitting in lawn chairs. True to their word, the soda sellers just had their signs out and there were vendors. There were also lots of paper cups with the familiar red and white Coca-Cola logo.

The best part, though, was that no one complained. It was as if the whole group, at least everyone at the picnic, accepted the signs and the logos as normal. It was the way life went in the 21st century. Pastor was even surprised at the number of people who came through the church crowd to buy soda, but who weren't with the church. He began to wonder if maybe there should be some kind of evangelistic message put on those red and white paper cups along with the corporate logos. He giggled to himself with possible slogans: "Have a Coke and a Savior," "Jesus is the only thing better than Coke," or "Jesus, the other real thing."

The next month when the board met, everyone marveled at how the extra cash from the profit stream—that is what they called it—at the picnic had helped keep everything floating. No cuts, not layoffs, and best of all no hard decisions. They were so pleased, the governing board of Old First Church created a special subcommittee in charge of seeking new ventures and new partnerships with corporate sponsors to help create other profit streams.

Pastor smiled, but he also worried. Something wasn't right, but he couldn't stop it. Everyone thought this was such a great idea and now all the folks were saying what a genius he was to help 'lead the church into the next wave of church stewardship.' It didn't feel like stewardship at all to Pastor. It felt like compromise.

But onward the plan went.

Within two months Verizon had placed a cell tower conveniently behind the steeple cross. The tower was so strategically placed it could only be seen from the third floor of the apartments two blocks over. On a more beneficial note, everyone got better reception and the dead zones in the church basement went away. This made being interrupted during potlucks much easier.

The telecommunications magnate had compensated heavily. They made a one time payment and agreed to monthly access payments to keep the tower in service. With some of the money received from that arrangement the board agreed it would give Pastor a nice big bonus.

Pastor had continued to worry about the whole idea of corporate sponsorship, but who can argue with a bonus. It actually felt really good to receive just compensation for work, for hard work in the care of souls. He socked all the money into his annuity knowing he would be wanting to retire soon. At this rate, the sooner the better. He didn't like the church of the 21st century. He didn't like where this was heading.

Two or three months after the Verizon contract was signed, Pastor was at home warming himself at fireplace as autumn's chill began to replace summer's warmth. He enjoyed gazing at the flickering embers of heat. It had always helped him to think. As he sat he sipped a particularly strong blend of black tea and pondered the path things were going. Two thoughts crossed his mind. One was what would the old heroes say about this. Not just Bible heroes, but folks like Milton, Spurgeon, or Barth? The second thought was like it; what will his grandchildren think of these financial arrangements?

Suddenly he noticed someone else was in the room with him. He looked up expecting his wife, but it wasn't her. It was an intruder. He was frozen with fear and couldn't move. Out of instinct he flung his tea cup at the darkly dressed man standing not 6 feet away from him.

The cup passed right through him and smashed against the wall.

Pastor gasped. He stood up and swung at the intruder but it was useless shadowboxing. He smote nothing but air.

"What?" he shouted as a half question and half swear.

"I am the Ghost of Church Past," said the specter.

"You've got to be kidding me."

"No kidding," replied the ghost. "Tonight you will have three visitors. I am the first. I am here to show you the church of the past."

Pastor noticed that the Ghost of Church Past looked familiar. Was this a trick? It couldn't be; the apparition looked exactly like his Greek professor from seminary. But the old linguistic theologian had been dead for fifteen years now. This was impossible.

Even as he pondered the impossibility of it Pastor realized he suddenly was somewhere else. It was a church, an old church with long wooden pews in it. Unpadded pews; which couldn't have been comfortable and the room was very cold. Everyone was wearing their coat while worshipping. No one looked like they were gong to the gym to swim. They looked like people who had made a sacrifice even to be at church.

Somehow he knew he was in the 1930's. The church was sparsely attended, mostly by women and children. The men who were there looked haggard and worn. At the front of the room the minister was beginning to speak. His old Greek professor, the ghost, said, "Listen to what they are working through, exegete this situation, son," and he extended his hand upward toward the lectern and the minister began to speak.

"I know times are tough, but there are people who have it tougher than us. We must find a way to keep the soup kitchen alive, or else people will go hungry. We're going to pass the offering plate again, and we know some of you have given and given, but we need more to keep the soup kitchen alive. This great and awful depression has hit us all, but some have been hit harder than others. We believe it is God's call upon us as his people to sacrifice for others. It is our duty to God and to man to give, even if it means to give till it hurts. Some of you grow some vegetables, if you have any of those please deliver them by noon tomorrow, or else some families will not have a dinner. Lives depend on it."

Pastor knew he was witnessing a hard pressed congregation with serious financial problems. He had read his history and understood it was churches who kept many people alive during the Great Depression through soup kitchens and bread lines. He never thought, though, how keeping those kitchens going must have meant a great sacrifice on the part of everyday parishioners. Parishioners who believed being unselfish and sacrificial was to be like Christ.

Immediately the scene changed around Pastor. Just as quickly as had been there in this old church, he now was in a fine, well appointed room. The wood was mahogany and the chairs all leather. There was a wet bar and decorative books lining an exquisite bookshelf. None of the books looked as if they'd ever been read. In the middle of the room sat an old stately desk. On one side sat a man he'd never seen, but on the other was his board member friend, Harry, who worked for the Coca-Cola Company. He knew instantly his friend Harry was talking to his boss back at corporate regional headquarters.

There was a third person in the room who looked completely out of place. He had short hair, tattoos all over his arms and neck, and was pierced above the eye, in the lip and in both ears. The tattooed man, who was in his mid-twenties, walked over to Pastor and said, "I'm the Ghost of Church Present. Listen at what they are planning."

Pastor was startled and stammered, "Where is my old Greek professor?"

The tattooed ghost said, "Shhhhh. He's finished. Listen preacherman."

At that admonition Pastor listened. He sulked a little and folded his arms around his chest to show his disapproval. He did not like this new ghost. Nevertheless, what he heard was fascinating.

Harry's boss smiled jovially and said, "Harry, you've done good work with this church thing. We were wondering, do you think you could get Old First Church to pry the edges off the entire denomination. If we could get a regional monopoly on all church functions for every church in the denomination within this region, we predict we can increase market share with the family values crowd at least twenty percent. I know it would be a lot of extra work, but corporate has put a high priority on this pioneer demographic. We think you're the best person for it, and if you pull this off a promotion is probably in store."

Harry nodded affirmatively and said, "You can count on me. My pastor is putty in my hands. We've thrown so much more money at him he is blinded by dollar signs. I think we can make this happen. I believe we can get the inside track on convention meetings, preaching events, and youth events. Sir, the key will be the music. If we can keep at this, say, for ten years then I believe we can begin to sponsor Christian music festivals and brand the next generation of church leadership. Then we can make inroads with the Lutherans."

The boss smiled broadly and exclaimed, "That's the spirit!"

They shook hands. The scene dissolved like a Hollywood fade out and now as the lights came up again Pastor sat in his own church. It was definitely his church, but everything was new and looked extremely updated, modern and professional. Sitting beside him, was him. It was the exact image of himself, except older. His doppelganger self said to him, "I am the Ghost of Church Future. Look at what you have done, look at what it has become."

With that he handed himself a piece of paper and Pastor opened it. It was a printed order of service, something like he had written up a thousand times. He began to read. The date was thirty years in the future. He scrolled down to see the following order of service printed as follows:

The Verizon "Call" to Worship
*   "Heavenly Sunlight" sponsored by Sunny Dee Citrus Drink*

Welcome (Today's Welcome courtesy of Frann's Espresso—where you're always welcome to the best cup of coffee on the east side)

The Daily Gazette Featured Announcements

First Lesson
*   Psalm 1 made possible by a grant from The Tree Farm Arboreal*

A Celebration of Baptism
*   Old First Church uses only Dasani Spring Water for its Holy Baptisms. If its pure enough for God's family, isn't it good enough for yours?*

Special Music
*   "I'll Fly Away" courtesy of American Airlines*

Children's Sermon made possible by contributions from Crayola Crayons

Second Lesson
*   1 Corinthians 13 (Hallmark reminds you, say "I love you" with a Hallmark card)*

Gospel Lesson
*   Matthew 14:13-21 "The Feeding of the Five Thousand"*
*   Gorton's Fish sticks is proud to sponsor Today's Old First Church Gospel Lesson*

Prayers for the Sick underwritten by Kleenex

The MGM Studios 'Roaring Lion' Morning Praise Song
*   "Lion of Judah"*

Sermon   "The Power of Positive Purchasing"

(Today's sermon is brought to you with limited interruptions by a special grant from your Baytown Chevrolet)

Pastoral Prayer Provided by St. Francis Regional Hospital

Holy Eucharist
    The Bread (baked especially for Old First Church by Orowheat)
    The Cup brought to you by Juicy Juice 100% pure grape juice

The Passing of the Peace courtesy of Shady Homes Funeral Services

Collection of Tithes and Offerings provided by Wells Fargo

Parting Hymn
    "Be Thou My Vision" sponsored by Pediatric Optometrists located on the corner of 6th and Seewell across from the mall

Benediction brought to you by ExxonMobile—We Go Where you Go!

A tear formed on his eye and ran down his cheek. His face became hot with sorrow and regret. How could he have let this happen? This was his doing. He created this monster.

At that he heard a sudden sound, and looked up to see the ministers walking in up on the chancel wearing their nice clean ministerial robes. He thought that odd because they never wore robes. This drew his attention away from his agony over hyper-commercialism. He looked very closely and noticed that where a cross should be on the stole, there was instead a Nike swoosh.

Righteous indignation rose in his throat. He could not contain himself any longer. He stood up, closed his eyes, balled up his fists and screamed, "This must end." When he opened his eyes he was again standing in front of his fireplace with a shattered teacup at his feet.

Steve Chooses

Steve obeyed the voices. He had always obeyed the voices, since he first heard them when he was seventeen. That is when they told him to run away from home. He obeyed the voices when they told him to stick the needle in his arm, because the needle made him feel good. He obeyed the voices that told him to drink hard liquor all day long. He obeyed the voices when they told him not to worry about getting a job. He obeyed the voices when they told him exactly how to steal from the convenience store. The voices were wise and smart.

Steve obeyed.

Sometimes he wondered why, but he never openly questioned the voices. The voices must be the sound of god, so he had to obey. He was special and god spoke to him directly through the gift of the voices.

So when the voices told him to get a handgun he didn't argue. He just did it. But it wasn't easy. Steve tried to buy one from a sporting good store. He asked the man behind the counter for a ".44."

The man behind the counter said, "I don't have one of those. Those are rare and hard to get. Who do you think you are Dirty Harry?"

"Well actually," Steve told the man, "that is what I had in mind. Do you know where I could get one?"

"Nope," replied the chubby man with a van dyke beard. He wiped his mouth with his flannelled sleeve and finished, "nobody around here will have one either. They are a collector's item. You could probably get one from an online site. You will not find one around here though; definitely not."

Steve walked out of that store despondent. He knew he had to obey; but where to get one.

He walked into the Callow Avenue Pawn Shop. There were rows of rings, necklaces, heirloom jewelry, knives, music CD's, DVD's, and hats, all behind glass. Steve stopped and looked at the shiny Zippo lighters. He always liked the Zippo lighters, especially the clinking sound they made when the lid was popped open. What he really liked was the smell of the lighter fluid. It reminded him of his father. In his memories of his father his dad smelled like Aqua Velva and lighter fluid. It was a funny memory as Steve had not seen his father since he was 6 years old. He didn't know why he was drawn to these antiquated lighters, but he had four of them.

There was one on the stand which had the emblem for the rock band AC/DC on it.

"That'd be so cool!" Steve shouted out loud.

But the voices scolded him. They demanded that he get back on task and stay focused. Steve must obey. He walked into the heart of the store and asked the tattooed and heavily pierced woman standing behind the glass case for the same thing he'd asked the flannelled man in the sporting good store; "I'd like a .44."

She looked at him and smiled. "Today is your lucky day."

"You've got one?" said Steve joyously.

"Nope. You won't find one of those anywhere except gun shows or a Hollywood studio shoot. Those are mostly collector's items. I've got something better. Something more stylish. It's a .357 magnum."

"Oh," he said. "Why would I want a .357?"

"Because you can do the same thing with a .357 that you want to do with a .44, except the .357 is cheaper and easier to carry. You do want to carry your gun, don't you?"

"Uh, yeah, I guess." Steve hadn't thought that far ahead. He didn't really know what he wanted the gun for. He could tell by the woman's demeanor that being able to carry the gun was desirable and something he should want to do. So he agreed and nodded at the woman.

"This one just came in yesterday," she said as she pulled a box from underneath the counter and opened it. "She's a sweet thing this one; the black steel and the wooden handle grips are a real turn on." She moved her index finger along the barrel of the pistol and caressed the hammer; and then fondled the trigger in a very suggestive way. She winked at Steve and said, "You know what I mean?"

Steve didn't know what she meant. She frightened him. He didn't know what she had in mind. Steve had never been very good with women and frankly didn't understand things like that at all. Some of the men at the feeding station were always talking about their 'Old Ladies' or their 'Woman' but their talk confused him. Steve didn't need any woman or old ladies. All he wanted to do was to make the voices happy. He lived for the voices.

The voices told him to get the gun.

"I'll take it. Don't worry about boxing it or anything."

The woman smiled. "You can't have it now, you'll have to fill out a federal background check and come back in seven days to pick it up. But I can think of some ways we can kill some time while we wait, if you know what I mean."

Steve didn't know what she meant. He wanted the gun now. He didn't have time for games; the voices would not wait. He had to get it this week. Steve didn't know why he knew that; he just did. He had to get the gun this week.

"I do not have time for this. Is there anything I can do to speed it up?"

"Uh," long pause, "No!" said the woman defiantly. "You wouldn't want me to break the law, would you?" She winked at him playfully as she said this. She continued, "There are tons of laws about handguns. I mean, this is a hock shop and all, but we still have to follow the law. We don't want to get shut down or nothing. Besides, we'd be responsible if you went off and did something crazy like killed people or something. Just be patient. You'll have to wait the same amount of days regardless of where you buy it. Besides, you will not find it for a better price anywhere."

Steve turned around and walked out.

"Hey, where are you going? Don't you want to wait with me?"

No, he didn't. He had to get a gun and fast. But where?

Steve sat at the plastic six foot table set up in the Salvation Army dining hall and slurped his stew and gnawed his hard dinner roll. As he ate, he worried about where to get a gun. The voices were not happy with him. They told him to hurry; time was running out.

Steve looked across at Willie. Willie was also eating his hard dinner roll and slurping his stew. Steve had known Willie for a while as they both dined at the Salvation Army almost every evening. He didn't really know anything else about Willie, but Willie seemed nice enough, and Willie was streetwise.

"Do you know where I can get a gun?" The question came off Steve's lips before he realized it.

"Yeah. Why?"

"Oh, I don't know. I think I just want one."

"Hey, I don't care, man. Just don't shoot me wif it," Willie smiled. His big white grin gleamed against the backdrop of his ebony face and scruffy beard. "How much do you got? That is the first question. Guns aint cheap, that's for sho."

"Well, I have $72.84. Is that enough?"

Willie replied, "Maybe. The second question is when do yous need it?"

"Now."

"Now?" Willie shouted. "Hey bro, chill. Lemme finish my stew first. I haven't eaten all day."

Steve watched nervously as Willie took what seemed like hours to finish his stew.

Finally they threw away their paper plates and sporks and walked out of the shelter into the cold, biting rain. It was now dark on the city streets and the weather was getting foul. Steve didn't know where he was going, he was just following Willie. It was not as if Steve had any other plans for the evening. After all, these were both homeless men.

Willie meandered across five city blocks to a part of town Steve rarely visited. The city was not very big, but it was cut into distinct, definite districts. Steve lived his life in the down and out but harmless hobo haunts. In pursuit of a handgun, Willie had taken them across 12th Avenue and into the drug gangland. The buildings here were not businesses. They were two and three story boarded up buildings. Once upon a time these had been nice apartments or department stores in the heart of the city. Now, they were a jungle of inner city blight left behind by a fleeing middle class.

Steve didn't think of any of that. He just kept wondering how much further until they reached the gun.

The duo rounded a corner and ducked into the smashed out front door of what was once a small grocer. They crossed through the storefront into the backroom where a short fat man with pasty white skin was sitting alone at a table. He was playing solitaire and drinking bourbon under the dim light of a single bulb burning overhead.

"Ray. My friend here needs a gun."

"Who is your friend?"

"My name is Steve. Do you have a gun?"

"Maybe," said Ray without looking up from his cards. "What kind of gun do you need?"

"I was told I probably should get a .357 magnum. Do you have one of those?"

"Yep."

"Can I have it?"

"Nope."

"Why?"

"Because you haven't paid yet. A .357 will cost you $150. Do you have $150?"

"No. I only have $72.84."

Anger and frustration swelled up inside Steve. Why was this so hard? Why couldn't he just get the stupid gun and make the voices happy? Why did it cost so much? Why did he have to get a gun in the first place?

Steve clinched his fists and showed his frustration. His cheeks turned red and his head shook violently as he screamed, "I must get a gun!"

"Relax," commanded Ray. "You'd better keep your cool. There are other people in this building and they are not as understanding as I am. Besides, you didn't say you just needed a gun. You said you needed a .357. I have other handguns."

With that Ray reached into his heavy army green coat and grabbed a Glock 9mm Compact and placed it on the table.

The voices in his head became ecstatic: "GET IT. BUY IT. OWN IT. USE IT. NOW!" they all said to him. He plopped down his entire wad of money onto the table and grabbed the gun quickly.

"BULLETS!" screamed the voices; their scream penetrating down into what little soul Steve had left.

"I need bullets too. Where can I get those?" Steve was so excited to finally have the gun he almost shouted the question.

"Wal-Mart. But there are already seven or eight rounds in the magazine to sweeten the deal. I have more if you want more."

"*Good. Plenty. Good*," whispered the voices.

Steve stuck the gun inside his coat pocket and walked out of the abandoned grocery store. His joy at satisfying the voices gave him a euphoric high. He became unaware of Ray or Willie. He smiled a stupid smile as he walked back through town toward the men's shelter where he spent cold winter nights. Steve was so elated that he didn't even notice the cold rain whipping over him.

The odd part about his joy is that it was not focused on the handgun. He did not fondle the gun, hold the gun, play with the gun, count the bullets in the chamber, aim the gun, or even clean the gun. Nothing about his behavior was even focused on the gun itself. He hadn't even noticed there was a bullet in the chamber.

His exuberance came from satisfying his masters. They were allowing him a moment or two of peace. They had loosened their talon's grip upon his nerves and their barking voices had gone away. They were happy. Now Steve could be happy.

He celebrated his good fortune by sharing the bottom half of a fifth with a woman named Amber in the alley behind the 4th Street McDonald's. Steve and Amber drank together often. Amber liked drinking with Steve because he always wanted to sit and talk, or as it were, sit and listen. Steve didn't say much but Amber always had a lot to say. Steve was not like the other men who always wanted something else from Amber. It was enough for him to sit by her under the building's awning to stay warm and drink from their common homeless communion cup together.

Amber was a lot like Steve. She had runaway from home and forsaken her past. Unlike Steve, she lived totally on the streets and never used the shelters. Having grown up in the area, she knew her way around better than most of the street people who were all from somewhere else. She and Steve had become drinking buddies. It was in this very alley, only two months ago, that Amber told Steve her secret. She had recently started hearing voices.

The night ended for Steve as he crawled into the shelter bed wet, dirty, and reeking of Jack Daniels. But he was at peace. As he closed his eyes to sleep sweet dreams, they shouted into his memory again one word.

"TOMORROW!"

The next day found Steve on the number seven bus. It was a rainy, winter, Sunday morning. The bus was empty except for two other men.

Steve knew both from the shelter. Riding the bus was one of the few true joys in Steve's life. When he rode he didn't have to think; he could just sit. No one would bother him; no one would come along and make him move. No one stared at him.

The bus just kept moving.

The driver was always nice.

It was always warm and dry.

He sometimes met friendly people.

He also loved the smell of diesel exhaust. Something about it made him think of his father.

But like life, and all good things, the bus ride must end. This particular bus ride ended at the third stop on Rhododendron Drive. That was where Steve was going. He exited the bus and stepped back from the road into the muddy ditch. Leaving the bus to re-enter the cold, wet, uncertain world was like a baby leaving the womb.

He held in his hand a small map for his journey. He had cut it out of the Yellow Pages ad. The map was small and crude, but it showed exactly how to get to Mosaic Community Church. That is where the voices told Steve to go.

From his crude map Steve determined that the church was about a mile up the road. He had never been to this part of town before, so he didn't know for sure. This world was different from his world. It was a clean residential neighborhood. All the lawns were perfectly manicured with flowerbeds and birdbaths. Many had two and three car garages. Most properties were clearly defined with decorative yard fences or elegant masonry.

On his pilgrimage to the church Steve saw a blue rambler with a wrap around porch and a dog in the yard. It was almost identical to the home he grew up in. He smiled as he walked by, yet the smile faded as the voices reminded him that was a lifetime ago. His childhood was over. He belonged to them now.

Steve accepted this and moved on. He was ready to get it over with; although he didn't yet know what "it" was.

Finally, he spotted the spire of the church building. The parking lot was full.

The voices told him to go inside. He did.

He entered through the west entrance and discovered himself in the middle of a moving throng of people. A woman approached him. She smiled and said, "I'm Wanda, you must be new to Mosaic?"

Steve shook his head up and down but didn't say anything. He was too overwhelmed with the mass of humanity to process verbal communication.

Wanda continued, "Let's get you a visitor's nametag and a cup of coffee. Do you like coffee?"

"Yes," Steve managed to reply.

"Follow me."

She took him by the arm and gently led him through the maze of men and women down two hallways and into a room labeled "Welcome Center."

"How do you take your coffee?" Wanda asked.

"Ah, black. I like it black." It had been a long time since anyone had asked him how he preferred anything. It felt good to be treated like this.

"Do you want a sticky bun? Pamela made these this morning. They are so good."

"Sure, I'd like that." Steve was slowly acclimating to this alien environment.

Steve sipped his coffee and ate his sticky bun and listened to Wanda talk. She was an older woman, about fifty-six or fifty-seven years old with bifocals on her face. She was wearing a grey sweater with a black skirt. Her hair was also grey, which gave her a smart looking color coordinated flare. As she talked her hands moved wildly and excitedly. She was talking about her church.

"We are so glad you decided to visit Mosaic Church this morning. You know, not too long ago we were called Third Extra Reformed Covenant Church. You might have heard of us by that name."

Steve nodded side to side indicating, "No" and thought he couldn't even pronounce that name. He just kept sipping his delicious coffee and munching his sticky bun.

"Well anyway, we were an itty bitty, dying church out here in the middle of nowhere. I know, brother, I was here. There was nothing going on and no one was coming into the church at all, I mean we were almost dead. Then God took over and changed everything. We started by changing our name. We thought Mosaic Church represented more who we wanted to be; represented more of our future than our past. We're still reformed and all, I guess, but it doesn't matter. We want to be open about our relationships with each other and God and not hide behind big frightening names. Don't you agree?"

Again, Steve nodded, this time up and down.

"Looking back, I know it took a long time, but it seems like it started happening so fast. At first a few new faces trickled in, but then as we updated our ministry programs, began looking out to our community, and engaged the local schools for ministry, well, tons and tons of young families came swooping in. Of course, we know it was God who did it, but I know that he used our new pastor to make most of these changes. In fact, most of our growth happened just after our new pastor arrived."

"PASTOR!" screamed the voices inside Steve's head.

"PASTOR! FIND HIM! HE'S THE ONE!" they ordered him.

Steve was startled. For the last few precious moments he had forgotten about the voices.

"Shoot," said Wanda. "I almost forgot to get you your nametag. Let's see, I have a marker here, what's your name?"

"Steve."

"Is that with a v or a ph?"

"Uh, v. Where can I meet this pastor."

"Oh, in about five minutes the 10:00 A.M. worship service starts. I think you should go to that service and then afterwards he always greets people out in the foyer. That is a fancy word that just means hallway outside of the sanctuary. Does that sound good?"

"YES!" the voices screamed.

"Yes," Steve answered Wanda.

"Then let's go," she said as she slapped his nametag on his chest and again, gently led him by the arm through two corridors and up a flight of stairs into the sanctuary of Mosaic Church.

Outside of a large doorway Wanda handed Steve over to an overweight man wearing a sport coat and buttoned down blue pinstriped shirt. He looked dignified with his black skin, graying cotton look to his hair, and wire rimmed glasses. The man smiled and handed Steve a piece of paper. Steve didn't know what to do with the paper so he crammed it into his pocket and smiled back at the man. The man said, "Let me help you find a seat. This is our crowded service and it might be hard to find a place to sit."

"Okay. But I don't have any money. Is there anyway I can get in free today?"

The man giggled. "Son, it doesn't cost anything to go to church; in fact, it pays to go to church." He paused and looked at Steve and then added, "You've never been to church before, have you?"

"No. Never. This is all so weird to me. I like it, but it is weird."

"That's okay. Someday I'll buy you a cup of coffee and tell you my story. I was about your age when I came to church for the first time too. It was at that time in my life that Jesus changed everything about me. He loves you, you know?"

"No, I don't know."

"Well, he does. I hope you discover that. Now, let's find that seat."

Again Steve found himself being navigated through a sea of humanity. Finally they found an open spot on the right hand side near the front of the sanctuary. Steve was sitting between two different families. On his right was a mother with two young children; a little girl and a little boy. On his left were a mother, father, and two teenage boys.

The little girl kept smiling at Steve, like she was playing a game of peek-a-boo. Steve tried not to smile back, but he could not help himself. He thought for a moment that the mother might pull her child back. That is what usually happened whenever Steve saw small children at the grocery store, on the sidewalk or on the bus. Parents always pointed at him and whispered to their children.

That didn't happen here. The young mother looked at Steve and said, "She has never met a stranger. I think she might grow up to be a missionary. She has a love for people. Now my son, he's a private one. He takes after his father."

"His father?" Steve asked innocently.

"Yeah, his father is in Afghanistan. We were all alone until we found Mosaic. It is really tough raising children by yourself. Here we connected with people struggling like us and got involved in a small group and the children just love their Bible classes. In many ways this place has become like family to us. Isn't family great?"

Steve did not know what to say.

"What is your story, what is your church background," she asked as she leaned forward to look at his visitor badge, "ah, Steve, yeah Steve. Did you grow up in church?"

He was just about to say, "No," when music came swooshing over the sanctuary. A drummer had begun tapping out notes and was quickly joined by a couple of guitars and a keyboard. A female vocalist began to sing. As she began to sing, everyone in the room stood spontaneously and began to sing with her.

This action frightened Steve and he jumped. He began to squirm and look all around for a way out. Suddenly a hand was on his shoulder. It was the father of the two teenage boys to his left. The man leaned over and said, "Its okay. Its only music. Relax. This is normal. We do this every week. Enjoy it."

That calmed Steve down a bit. The music was nice. The woman was singing about Jesus and how he was the "Prince of Peace." The group sang for about twenty minutes; moving from one song to another. The words were projected on a large screen but that didn't help Steve much. He had never heard any of this kind of music before and he couldn't keep up. But the man was right. It was nice. It was far different from anything he'd thought about church. Somehow in his mind he'd always envisioned old men sitting around a big table talking about how bad everyone in the world was. He'd never thought people at church might treat him with kindness.

As the music faded and the band walked away, a tall man with shocking curls of blond hair walked onto the platform.

"HIM!" the voices shouted inside Steve's head. The voices were so loud he looked around to see if anyone else heard it. They didn't. They were all paying careful attention to what the man on the platform was saying.

The man said a short prayer and then looked out to the audience and said, "Welcome to Mosaic Church, I'm Pastor Adam and we're glad you are worshipping Jesus with us today. Today I want to talk to you about the love of God. There is no greater force in the universe than the love God has for each one of us. Yes, he loves the whole world, the collective humanity, but that does not diminish at all his incredible love for each one of us as individuals; by name, as people with personalities." As Pastor Adam said this, he was looking right at Steve.

"SHOOT HIM!" the voices screamed.

"Now?" Steve said aloud.

The young mother beside him whispered, "Yes, God loves you right now, just the way you are, Steve."

Steve was very confused. The voices increased their repetitive chant,

"SHOOTHIMSHOOTHIMSHOOTHIMSHOOTHIMSHOOTHIM!"

"No," said Steve bravely under his breath, "I will not."

"*Yes, you will. You have too. We own you. You have no choice, you belong to us.*" The voices were again seducing Steve with their twisted persuasion. Steve had always obeyed the voices and they had led him through so much. He knew he belonged to them and he must obey. But he didn't want to.

Meanwhile, Pastor Adam kept talking on the stage. "Everyone has a choice as to whether or not he or she will receive this gift of God's love.

That is the beautiful thing about us; we each have free choice within the context of God's sovereign plan. It is his will that everyone be loved and receive love—the Bible calls that saved. But each of us must choose whether or not we will live in the joy of that love. As a Father loves a child, so the Father of all loves us all. As a husband loves a wife, so God loves us. We each have to live in that love."

"LIES!" the voices shouted angrily. Then their tone changed back to their seductive whisper; "No one loves you. There is no such thing as love. You have no choice; we are your god. Do as we say. We brought you here, remember. Did you like the coffee, did you like the sticky bun? We brought you to that. Did you like the nice people? We brought them to you. Did you like the bus ride? We provided that for you. Show your gratitude and shoot him."

Steve had always obeyed the voices.

He pulled out the crumbled paper from his pocket and wrote, and then he stood up and stepped through the crowded row of faithful worshipers. The little girl smiled at him one more time. The father of teenagers gave a polite smile as he turned sideways to let him by. Soon Steve was in the aisle. An usher was up in a moment and whispered "the bathrooms are out those doors and to your left," as he pointed to the back of the sanctuary.

Steve ignored him and turned toward the platform.

The distance was not far, only about thirty feet or so. Most people in the sanctuary saw Steve stand up and were watching, wondering what was going on. Steve was oblivious to their stares or curiosity. Pastor Adam kept talking, but had turned his gaze toward Steve and smiled at him. Another usher popped up and whispered to Steve, "Are you okay?"

Steve replied, "Yes." Then he took seven more steps and put his hand inside his coat pocket—his brown stained and soiled coat, the coat which had been both blanket and pillow and now was armory. He pulled out the handgun with the partial magazine clip. In one motion he lifted it up and pointed it at Pastor Adam and pulled the trigger.

The bullet ripped right through Pastor Adam's blue sports blazer, into his shirt and piercing his chest. The bullet went straight to his heart and exploded his cardiac muscles before it exited through his shoulder blade and hit the large wooden cross which was mounted behind the church's platform.

The voices shrieked with joy and their joy gave Steve a moment of peace. Then they squealed inside his mind, "SHOOTHIMAGAIN!" Steve squeezed off another shot, this one missed Pastor Adam and lodged into the sheetrock wall.

Screams were heard throughout the building. People began running in every direction, looking for cover. Worshipers became wailers. Adam's wife was sitting on the front row and she instinctively ran to her husband.

"SHOOT HER TOO!" the voices yelled at Steve and obediently he pointed the gun at her as she ran to her husband's side. She never saw Steve; all she saw was her fallen husband.

A third shot rang out, but this one didn't come from Steve's gun. It was from an off duty police officer who worshiped at Mosaic church who was sitting on the third row. His shot found its target. It burst through Steve's forehead and exploded out the back of his skull.

The Pastor's wife grabbed her husband by the hand but she was unable to speak and too shocked to cry. She'd never imagined anything like this before. It was completely outsider her realm of thought; even the dark dreadful imagination people try and forget about as ever being possible.

The dying pastor looked at his wife and uttered, "Elaine, I love you." Then he gazed up toward heaven and asked the eternal question which surrounds all tragedy.

"Why?"

Then he died in his wife's arms.

The whole incident was over before anyone really knew what had happened. 911 calls flooded the police and soon emergency vehicles were all over the church parking lot. Local television stations sent their film crews and helicopters out to the suburban church to broadcast the tragedy. Their images failed to capture the key story of the event. They were only able to broadcast the aftermath of crying, angry, and grieving parishioners.

The newspaper the next day informed the world with the headline, "Local Pastor Killed by Homeless Vagabond." The newspaper missed the true story, however. Two victims were killed that day. Both were murdered by the voices.

Prayer Request

The worship center was very warm for this Sunday evening service. The small crowd of the usual suspects sat in their usual spots fanning themselves in the usual way. The sanctuary felt like a cave. Hours before it had held hundreds, but now only a handful were present.

Few people attended the anachronistic service. The church had maintained it as a care ministry to a dying generation who thought it so vital. Actually, they maintained it because the pastor was too spineless to get rid of it. The political price to be paid for ending it could have cost him his job. So he went along with these aging powerbrokers because he knew, regardless of what Dan Brown or anyone else speculated, these were the true *Illuminati* who made the decisions for the world.

The primary attendees were women who were either widowed or who had husbands which were less spiritual than they were. At least, that is how their wives felt about it. The only two or three men who ever attended were those whose wives badgered them into coming.

But tonight the only man in the room was the pastor.

He stood in the center aisle with his lectern ready. He was winded from leading a half dozen old hymns played with choppy rhythm on an old piano badly in need of tuning. As was his tradition, before he started his lesson on the "Parable of the Soils" in Matthew 13, the pastor took prayer requests.

The first request was about an upcoming knee surgery for a daughter. They prayed. The second request was for a dear saint who was recovering from hip surgery in a local convalescent home. They prayed. The third request was for a soldier serving overseas whose wife had left him. They prayed. The fourth request was for a friend who had been diagnosed with terminal cancer. They prayed.

Then Miss Ayers began making her requests. The pastor knew the prayer needs would be coming off in groups because she always made her requests in groups. The elderly woman rattled them off in her unique sing-song speech pattern. She said, "Well, pray for me that I get my new eyeglasses soon because I'm not seeing all that well. I have an appointment next month to see the eye doctor. Also, pray for my husband as he is having cataract surgery on one eye in about ten days and then they will do the other one in about seven weeks. Finally in two weeks we are driving through Oregon down into Northern California to see our family who we haven't seen in months."

For a moment there was a pause in the room. The pastor drank in what he had just heard. Then he laughed out loud at the logical conclusion of two blind people in their eighties driving across some of the most rugged terrain in all the lower forty-eight. Then he realized he was the only one laughing. Everyone else thought it completely normal.

The prayer meeting continued; although the pastor fought back the giggles for the rest of the night. On the spot, though, he changed his Sunday evening lesson from the Parable of the Soils to The Blind Leading the Blind.

Fifty Miles an Hour

Fifty miles an hour.

That is Ben's speed as he drives the city street. The cityscape flies by with its designer coffee shops and the many other pock marks along the street: Arco. Asian Cuisine. Old big churches with digital reader signs. McDonalds. In the distance the only essence of elegance is the beautiful mountain which hangs from the heavens.

But it all looks pretty much the same at fifty miles an hour.

Ben pulls into the Fifth Street Parking Garage. He weaves his Prius through the first two levels of parking and finally finds a spot on the top level between a Chevy Truck and a Volkswagen Jetta. As he makes his way toward the entrance of the municipal hospital, he walks briskly past the valet he had ignored, and moves in through the glass door to the entrance.

He pauses for a moment to get his sense of direction straight. Hospitals all look the same from the outside, but this hospital was like Pan's Labyrinth on the inside. Yet, Ben knows his way around this particular hospital better than most. It all comes back to him rather quickly as he navigates easily through the corridors. All he needs to do is figure out exactly where he needs to go.

He takes an elevator up one floor, down the hallway, and passes the oncology wing, and through the dining hall where early lunches are being eaten and mid-morning snacks nibbled.

A dozen years ago he had been one of those sitting in hard plastic chairs in the midst of this sanitized bastion of healing. On that day, years ago he had hoped that the doctors who wore the blue priestly robes of medicine actually knew what they were talking about. Walking through the lunch area this morning he glimpsed faces, and with each glimpse he tries to guess what they might be here waiting and praying for. A heart transplant? A brain tumor? Chemotherapy?

Twelve years ago he sat there and wondered, "Will my child live?" Were any here today thinking the same thing? Moving past the cafeteria he knows some had to be thinking that for the largest children's wing in the state is right here, the best doctors in the region are upstairs right now working miracles. Or trying to, that is, while the people down here are praying for one.

With every step he remembered so much. Each step was a painful reminder of ancient trauma he'd prefer to forget. His effort is unsuccessful. He had to face the reality that coming here was to stroll again down the hallways of dashed hopes.

Nevertheless, he still hopes today, for John's sake, that the doctors know what they are doing. John's room is his destination, and is located through the refectory and onto another elevator and up to the fourth floor. K Wing. ICU.

When the elevator car opens the room ahead is full of people. Black people. Asian people. Native American people. White people. Blind people. People. Hurt is not a racist and it does not discriminate. Disease does not check your ethnicity or religion. Everybody gets sick. Everybody dies. Everyone cries.

He walks to the left because that was the only option. To the right is a wall with pretty pictures of butterflies, daisies, mountains, salmon and airplanes. Emotional sanitizer for the virus called reality. It is odd, Ben wonders, how everyone thinks it is some kind of illness to feel depressed. He mumbled, "Are these pictures supposed to make me feel better about being here?" There is nothing not depressing about ICU.

He thinks about all the ICU's he's been in during his work. Probably over a hundred, he guesses, from all over the country, and they all feel the same. It does not matter if it is a civilian hospital, military hospital, Jewish hospital, Catholic hospital, County hospital or Plush hospital. ICU means one thing and everyone knows it. ICU means almost dead. If things go bad in ICU the next room is the lobby of the funeral home.

But then again, funeral homes are always sanitized with pretty pictures too.

He walks down the hall to the double doors with the phone hanging on the wall. He lifts the phone and punches button #1. Faceless Anonymous Voice states, "ICU" as if Ben doesn't know where he is. "I'm here to visit John Moorehead. I believe he is in this ICU wing. May I see him?"

"Just a moment." As he waits, Ben hears keystrokes.

"Sure, come on through the double doors," says Faceless Anonymous Voice. Ben pushes hard to get the mechanical doors open and there is another room full of people. These people are not patients.

It is an all female group, all wearing bright pink and blue nurse's shirts. Some kind of tour is going on and it is very noisy in the ICU.

433, that was the number John was in. The door opened to 451. Ben snakes around the corner looking for Faceless Anonymous Voice who had guided him through the hallway phone. Faceless Anonymous Voice is nowhere to be seen or heard. Maybe she exists at a switchboard in the basement and doesn't actually work in ICU. He makes eye contact with a short blond woman. "Hi," he said, raising his voice above the dull roar of the tour. "Is it okay if John Moorehead has a visitor? He is in bed 433."

"Let me see," comes out of her mouth as she quickly walks away. She looks doubtful and worried. Maybe Faceless Anonymous Voice had been too hasty in granting him access. Maybe John can't have any visitors today.

She returns quickly enough, though, and says, "Yes. He is in bed 433. I'll show you the way." Ben almost says, "I know he is in bed 433, I am the one who told you that!" but he doesn't. He realizes he is just on edge and irritated. So he practices controlling his tongue and instead just follows her.

She is a fast walker.

As with most ICUs there are no doors. The curtain hangs from end to end on a track. Every bed has its curtain open. Some of the patients are moaning. Many are asleep. The majority have big machines plugged into their bodies. The machines make a lot of noise. It is very loud in the ICU, much louder than the tour of pink and blue nurses.

Some of the hoses are connected to big boxes with digital lights and numbers that flash and change intermittently. Some connect to poles with bags of fluid. Some fluid is red. Some fluid is golden yellow. Some fluid is clear. Some is dark. Bile, blood, urine, and saline are the paints on God's palette. From these fluids comes the stuff of life and death. If the wrong color goes into the wrong bag at the wrong time people die.

The thing Ben notices—today and always at ICU, is that the patients have no visitors. The only comfort suffering people have is the loud machines and the bustling health care professionals. There is no beauty here.

The pretty pictures of salmon, airplanes and daisies should be in here, not in the elevator lobby where the healthy are. The elements of beauty ought to be in the rooms where the sick are. Ben thought for a moment as he followed fast walking woman that beautiful men and women should be hired by hospitals to sit by the beds of sick people to tell beautiful stories. Mozart should be played loud enough to drown out the noise of the respirators.

Prints of Renaissance paintings should be hung.

None of that is here nor in any ICU he'd ever seen. There is no music, no beautiful storytellers, no Renaissance prints. There is not even *Dogs Playing Poker* on the wall. Only the technical is found here, as if human beings were only machines. The only things worse than ICUs was nursing homes. Nursing home day was Thursday.

433. John is laying on the rotating bed which keeps him moving because he can't. His head is big, much bigger than it should be. There is a jagged set of stitches across his face beginning on his left jaw and moves over his nose and up over his right eye to his where his scalp begins. His leg is bandaged. There is a thick brace around his neck. There are no blankets or covers on him. He is asleep.

Bubbly attendant nurse asks Ben who he is. He tells her. She says John is a nice man. He will get better, she says. "He can hear you if you talk to him," she assures.

"How can he," thinks Ben, "over all this noise." A loud machine is three feet from his head.

Ben approaches the side of the bed and takes John's left hand. The hand is hot with fever. He tells John that his friend Sam found out he was in the hospital. He talks about the work on the garage. He shares a story or two about Sunday. He mentions the sermon and how that went, and speaks about how a couple of little old ladies had squabbled about something in the breakfast ministry. John always enjoyed hanging around the breakfast ministry so Ben thinks that might cheer him up; if John can actually hear him.

Ben does not talk about the accident.

He doesn't have that much to say. What can be said? This is a one way conversation.

There is a long pause. Ben weeps. John doesn't move or stir.

Then Ben prays. He asks that God heal John; that he take away his pain and quickly restore his health so that he can get back to doing the things he loves. He prays out loud and as the "Our Father" rolls off his tongue Ben's voice quivers and then breaks. He opens his eyes and looks at John's broken face, the stitches, the tracheotomy, the tubes, and the fevered hand. He squeezes the fevered hand, the unresponsive grip and he hears his own heart beat and he doesn't want to pray this prayer anymore. All he wants to talk to God about is, "Why?"

But Ben knows better. He knows John is lucky to just be alive. He knows why this happened. John was walking on the side of the road and did not see the car traveling fifty miles per hour in a thirty zone. It hit him, and sped away, leaving him for dead.

What Do You Want Me To Do, Mom?

"Do you want Dad's gold wedding band?"

The older woman to whom the question was directed sat still, holding a blue tissue in her left hand and a pair of reading glasses in the other. She seemed to not hear the question, so her middle aged, rotund son asked it again.

"Do you want Dad's gold wedding band?"

This time she gave a glance and brought the tissue to her nose.

"I don't know. What do you think, Kevin?" she asked in response. Kevin responded in kind and put the question back to his mother. "That depends on what you want, mom."

Again, she sat still, unmoving and silent.

The seconds built into minutes and it felt as though she sat there an hour pondering that one question: "Do you want Dad's wedding band?" To her the seconds were not nearly long enough. They were precious and painful seconds, those moments when her husband had breathed his last breath, and with a spasm left the earth another victim to the black plaque called cancer. She wanted more seconds to be with her husband.

Unlike his mother, Kevin felt the pressure of time. He felt the need to explain the situation, again.

"I talked with Annie, the nurse on duty," Kevin continued. "She said if we want to get Dad's wedding band it would be better to do it before the funeral home showed up." He paused as the actions of what he just said were finally sinking in. His father had only been dead forty-five minutes. Kevin swallowed hard, and continued, "I can do that, if you want me too."

Mom just sat there. Her own demons began to haunt her now. For over two years she had slowly declined as Alzheimer's stole away memory after memory. Now, she was unable to stay in the moment and think about wedding bands. Alzheimer's had joined forces with a new ally called grief and together they were taking control of her thoughts. She looked at her son and began talking.

"It must have been three or so in the morning. I couldn't sleep so I went in there to see Donald. He was so thin and his eyes half opened. I guess I was the last person to see him. That means I was the last person he saw." These words do not pour out of her mouth; they slowly trickle in a soft, reflective Carolina accent.

Again, more silence. The forty-five minutes since she had learned of her husband's death had been filled mostly with silence and tears. Tears are the language of sorrow. Everyone is fluent in this mother tongue and translation is never needed. Words fail and sound shallow; even stupid. But tears are always appropriate for communicating sorrow. Only tears adequately convey the pain of loss, the anxiety of separation, and the nagging notions of fear.

Yet in this silence the old matriarch pushed back the tears. Now her enemy Alzheimer was helping her. He pushed her out of the present moment and into the past but with his own clever style of connected themes.

"You know I have Donald's other wedding bands," she smiled as she said it. "They are in the jewelry box by the night stand. Those were the wedding bands," she chuckled, "that I had to buy him when he gained all that weight. Donald surely did love to eat." Now her smile was growing and her very pronounced and southern accent was elongating as she was enjoying the thought. "His fingers got so fat from all the greasy food and sweets he enjoyed that his wedding ring was too small and too tight on his fat fingers. We had to buy him another set. They were his fat set. Oh how he loved pie."

She laughed. Kevin laughed. It felt good to have that memory. Kevin wondered how much longer his mother would have that memory before it too slowly slipped away.

No one would have the smile long because the thought of Donald as fat seemed preposterous now. Cancer had turned him into skin and bones. The last two months of his life were one trip to the hospital after another. The barbarism of radiation and chemotherapy had killed his appetite. He had been shrinking like wax melting against the heat of a flame.

Mom must have been thinking along the same lines. She said, "That was when I knew he was really sick, when we took his fat rings off."

Kevin asked the question again. "Do you want me to get Dad's gold wedding band?"

The aging woman mustered her considerable dignity and turned to her daughter-in-law Janet. "What do you think, dear."

"It depends, really," Janet said. Janet didn't have the automatic connection her husband did with his mother, so she carefully thought about the response. "If you want to hold it and remember it, then get it. But if you want to know that there is a symbol of your love which he takes to the grave, then leave it on his finger." Kevin looked at his wife, as if surprised at her gentle wisdom.

The newly ordained widow wiped her nose again with the same blue tissue paper. She sat in silence, meditating upon the question.
She remembered the altar where the vows were made, "till death do us part." What a cruel joke that the happiest day of her life would have mention of this, the saddest day of her life.

She remembered slipping the ring nervously over his finger. She thought of him playing with the ring, twirling it between his fingers like he did when he was nervous.

The time he lost it chopping firewood made her angry all over again.

Suddenly with resolve she looked straight at Kevin, and said sternly, "I want you to get his watch. That's a nice watch."

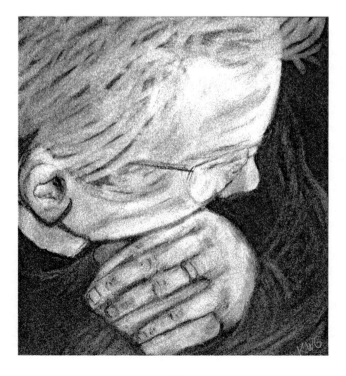

tempus fugit(ive)

where have the years gone?
some are smashed between
the cushions of the back seat.
a few are hidden in a yellowing
box labeled heirlooms: bridal
maybe? a couple are tucked safely
away between the pages of books.

where have the years gone?
they washed away with the meandering
stream on lazy summer jaunts. somewhere
they are stacked into neat
piles upon a mopped hardwood floor. one
year i'm sure is found waiting in the
lounge at the doctors office.

where have the years gone?
worry ate some years. useless, fretting
worry over what turned out to be nothing.
we spent some years worrying about money. there
will be no money in heaven, which is where we
will be when all the years are gone. it is likely there
will be money in hell (but nothing to buy).

where have the years gone?
some melted away in acrimonious hot anger. anger
which makes the cheeks red and blood pressure
rise. angry at people, work, the world: but I can't
remember for the life of me what we were angry
about.

where have the years gone?
some years died of boredom. duty and office
domesticated us. predictability sucked
all life out of us those days. this sucking left us
as space zombies roaming our own personal
cosmic graveyard.

where have the years gone?
many but not enough were digested by the
fruit of our loins. when they hatched

they were voracious for time,
attention, instruction, and play. but these are
good years. we enjoy feeding the begotten
ourselves. they will bury us.

where have the years gone?
passion's lunge grabbed its fair
share of years. it caressed the work of
words and lessons, smeared pigment
on canvas and wood, hummed along with notes and
lyre. most of all passion pulled us together
like magnets: helpers lovers pilgrims counselors
but most of all friends.

where have the years gone?
i can't say for sure—for time is un-
pre-dict-able. the good and bad years are
recorded upon the tablet of our hearts
for permanent keeping as we pass
into eternity.

Who Flushed?

"If you need to go to the bathroom, go now." These words came out of his mouth with a matter-of-fact candor that was unsettling.

"Why?" Aaron said.

"Because in five minutes I am tapping into your sewer main," the man shouted while pointing to the newly constructed house sitting just on the other side of the property line. This was all happening for no apparent reason.

It was early in the morning and Aaron had not even sipped his fresh poured coffee and this short man who was shaped like a gourd stood here giving him orders. This was the first interaction he had had with any human being all day and it was not what he expected. Indeed, if he had, the night before, made a list of all the things he would talk about first thing in the morning, fecal matter and flushing would not have been one of them. It wouldn't even have made the top one hundred.

After all, he had never seen this bossy man before. He certainly didn't know who he was and now the man had come barging into the quiet church kitchen unannounced. This unsettledness led to Aaron taking a defensive posture and he quickly shot back to the man, "Do you have a permit to do this?"

Aaron didn't know anything about permits except it seemed one needed a permit to do most anything, and he figured tapping into the church's sewer main would be one of them.

The gourd shaped man replied with a sideways cocked grin, "What do you think?"

Aaron was still defensive and wanted to say, "I think I want you to answer yes or no. It is not hard—one is a two letter answer and the other is a three letter answer. One of those should be the right answer. You only have five letters to choose from." But those words didn't come out of his mouth. He chose to hold his tongue.

The house the irritating man was pointing to was to be his neighbor, and somewhere deep inside Aaron a sermon came to mind, a sermon which once came out of his mouth about being nice to your neighbors, even if they are not nice to you. Keeping this in mind, Aaron said, "Easy, I was just wondering. We want to be good neighbors. So, we won't flush." He said these words while holding his hands out in an open, affirming gesture. He had learned this once in a communications theory book. "How long do you think that will take?"

"About an hour," said the troll. "Are there any people here besides you?"

His nosiness was getting annoying. Aaron wanted the man to go away quickly and take his demanding demeanor with him.

"My administrative assistant will be here in a few minutes, and then some others, no more than five or six, will be in later. But tonight we will have—"

Oblong the Anonymous interrupted rudely, "I said we'd be done in an hour, didn't I? It won't take more than that." Aaron was miffed. His coffee trembled on the brim of the cup. He had been deprived of bragging that he had a thriving Wednesday Evening ministry which would be there tonight. Besides, this guy used questions like interrogative artillery to weaken any resistance to his intimidating, early morning rudeness.

The unnamed construction worker walked back to his green house and Aaron walked back to his study. He entered his door and murmured to himself, "The meek shall inherit the earth." As he worked he could hear all the pneumatic tools pounding at the home across the yard. Then there was the beeping backing backhoes and yelling voices shouting directions "to the left…a little to the right…Whoa!"

He couldn't stop being aggravated. He had lived with these noises for almost two full months and now these noises were spilling into his world and into his church's kitchen.

Two hours later Aaron's assistant walked down the hall and relayed a message from the foreman next door. She informed him, "We still can't flush because the city inspector hadn't arrived."

A big grin formed on Aaron's goateed face. It was inconvenient, but at least the oppressive tool-wielder had been wrong on his timeline.

Forty minutes later she again came down the hallway and updated Aaron on the situation. She said the Napoleon with the green vest told her to flush in five minutes so they could make sure the line was clear.

Unbelievable! Now this guy is giving Aaron's employees orders. Aaron wondered if Mr. Tool Time would show up Sunday to preach. Meek wasn't working.

A half hour later the as yet to be named bulldozer boss came running into the office building. He addressed his speech to no one in particular and just began talking, as if people were doing nothing but waiting for him to speak. But what he said was compelling.

"Why did you flush?" He asked the question with a high pitch in his voice. The sound of his complaining tones reminded Aaron of the sound effects from old World War II movies of bombs screaming toward their target.

"Who flushed?" asked the confused secretary. "We only flushed the one time when you asked us to so you could check the lines to make sure it was clear."

The still nameless man screeched, "Not the line clear; that was a half hour ago. Just now, not three minutes ago, someone over here flushed! Why? Who? Someone flushed over here!"

Aaron could tell his assistant was about to unload on this man. Her tolerance was less than even his. The pastor began to speak, "No one flushed over here. We are in latrine limbo waiting on you fellas. We've been that way all morning. You said it would only be an hour. We have done our best to help you out and I can tell you, no one over here flushed." Aaron said this with a tone of satisfaction. He knew that neither he nor his co-worker had flushed and there was no one else on the property.

"Well," the man paused, "someone did. We were standing in a five foot hole and suddenly out came sewer water. That wasn't nice."

"I'm telling you, we didn't do it." Aaron pepped up when he said it this time and was preparing himself to enter into another volley of words, but before he could finish and enjoy the full satisfaction of victory, the angry man left as quickly as he had come. Aaron wondered if this oaf had ever enjoyed a two-way conversation; or any conversation beyond simply barking at people.

Amusement turned to belly laugh as Aaron imagined if the God who parted the Red Sea and then let it loose in time to flood Pharaoh's army had not done the same thing on a septic scale. God flushed.

"Vengeance is mine," says the Lord.

Good Plague Stuff

I was preaching through the book of Exodus in the Hebrew Bible and needed something poetic, not prose, in an upcoming sermon to adequately summarize the ten plagues, Pharaoh's cold hard heart, and the Passover event. I also was looking for information that would put a definite Jesus spin on the events. I could not find anything to fit. Therefore I wrote my own.

A Psalm of Plagues

Bubbling out of the delta mud,
God's plague spewed blood;
turning the Nile into red,
"let my people go" he said.

Frogs, flies, boils, and hail,
the will of the Lord must prevail.
Pharaoh knows he cannot win;
doomed by plague number 10.

Swab the hyssop on the posts,
at midnight comes the Lord of Hosts.
Eat the herbs and unleavened bread;
plagued Egypt's firstborn falls dead.

Egypt is the world and all therein.
Plagues are punishment upon sin.
The blood is as Christ the Lamb;
sent to us by the great I Am.

Sunburn

In the summer of 2002 I was with our Youth Group at summer camp. The afternoon activity was Counselor Hide-N-Seek. The adults hide. The students seek. I took my writing book and climbed a tree in the woods. While I waited to be found, I reflected on the odd practice of sunbathing and wrote the following poem. I never was found, and after a couple of hours I came down for dinner.

Cookies, chicken, and fish bake;
but so do kids by the lake.
People without cover or hats,
use aloe balm in vats.

Perhaps long ago it fried;
their brains in the sun, dried.
It explains the absence of sunscreen
as they cook their little spleen.

"I'm okay, I'll tan"
a boy said as he ran.
I wondered in my mind whether
this boy was stage 1 leather?

Crazy folk roasting their midriff;
like lemmings going over a cliff.
From the Bible they must learn
where it says to turn or burn.

Amber Chooses

Amber woke up in the alley; which was usual for her. The rain, which started falling very slowly on this late Sunday morning now began to grow strong. As it did, it served as her alarm clock. The liquid sunshine was blowing back under the eaves from the buildings overhead onto her face. She wiped the crusted sleep from her eyes and stood up. Grabbing her backpack, she stumbled out of the alley and toward the thoroughfare.

She was hungry.

Amber couldn't remember her last meal.

Did whiskey count as a meal? If yes, then her last meal was last night with her friend Steve; if no, then it had been at least three days. She felt around in her pockets to see if there was anything to eat hidden in there. Sometimes she'd been known to stick a chicken leg or a Hot Pocket in her coat.

Nothing.

Did she have any money? She checked her blue jeans and heard change. She pulled it out. She had a couple of dollar bills and some loose change which came to a grand total of $3.53. Then she checked her backpack to see what might be in there. It was her lucky day. She found $1.66 in a side pouch. She sifted through the coins twice to make sure there was no Canadian money in there by accident. Two months ago she had somehow ended up with a handful of Canadian loons.

"Sweet," she whispered to herself as she smiled. All of this was United States "In God We Trust" money. Her grand total was $5.19. She felt rich. She did not know when she'd had that much money in a long time. It was now time for breakfast. But first, she needed to heed nature, so she stepped back into the alley and splashed the asphalt.

Feeling much better now, Amber walked up the boulevard and into the convenience store. With $5.19 she had a world of options. She could buy a soda, a bag chips, a breakfast biscuit, and still have money left over for a candy bar. Or, she could buy five packages of powdered donuts and drink water from the drinking fountain. She might even have enough for one of those prefab heat and eat pancake breakfasts under the deli counter.

"*Steal*," said the voices inside her head.

"*In coat, buy cigarettes.*" She hated the voices.

The first time she heard them, two or three months ago, she thought it was the Central Intelligence Agency attempting mind control. She still wondered if that might not be the case. But lately, she'd come to believe the voices were her own mind; that part of her which wanted to do wrong things. She self diagnosed the voices as schizophrenia based on the "Intro to Psychology" course in her freshmen year. Amber had studied for two years at the University before she ran away. She had been a very good student.

Nevertheless, she still figured the CIA was a possibility.

Usually she ignored the voices. They told her to do things she knew were wrong. As they were now, they were telling her to steal. Amber had thought about stealing, but she never did. She had slept with men for money, she had used drugs, she had lied to police officers and others to get what she wanted.

But she had never stolen.

Amber knew, though, that the voices were smart. They were telling her the old trick. Steal something with the left hand while paying for something with the right hand. If she buys cigarettes then the clerk will never suspect her of stealing. If, however, she just walks out without buying something; she is a suspect.

Amber refuses to steal. In fact, the voices make her angry and she yells out loud to the voices, "Go to Hell!"

They responded to her by giggling, and then they go away. Gone where, she did not know. She hoped to Hell.

The dirty street urchin then walked to the counter having made her dining choice. She bought a sausage biscuit, two powdered donuts, and a small coffee. She would save one of the powdered donuts for her friend Steve, whom she would probably see tonight. It was his

84

turn to bring the bourbon.

But Steve didn't show up that evening. She was tempted to eat the donuts she'd kept for him all day. But she didn't. Instead she panhandled for some coins and bought herself some cheap beer, the kind which comes in enormous pint bottles. She had enough to buy two of them. It wasn't enough to make her drunk, but it did make her comfortable. She sat in her alley underneath a makeshift cardboard hut to keep the soft Pacific Northwest rain off of her. She dozed off, surrounded by the familiar sounds of traffic and rustling Busch Beer cans rolling on the pavement at her feet.

Sometime around midnight Amber was startled awake. She could hear hurried footfalls in her alley. She had lived here for two years and had never felt threatened by any of the street people. But right now, she felt unsafe. "Who could this be?" she wondered.

"Amber," a voice cried out. It was a man's voice. At first she thought it was her buddy Steve. But it didn't sound like him at all. No, this voice seemed irritated, or, perhaps angry. No, not angry. It sounded authoritarian.

Amber tried not to move. She was certain that whoever it was would not see her in her cardboard hut because the alley was so dark. She took a chance and peeked out of the make-shift flap-door and got an eyeful of flashlight beam. Out of instinct she squinted and covered her eyes with her hand. At the same time she let out a yelp.

"Amber?" the voice yelled inquisitively.

Amber stood up and saw the unmistakable outline of a police uniform cast from the street lights. She also saw a man standing behind him in an overcoat. She couldn't see his face, but saw his coat.

"*RUN*" the voices shouted inside her head. For once, she agreed with them.

At that she took off like a spooked deer in the forest. She ran hard in the opposite direction, leaving her backpack and shopping cart behind. She hoofed it hard, not wanting to get caught by the CIA. In High School she had been on the basketball team and she used that agility to navigate this dark alley. This was her home and she knew it well.

She quickly darted to the opposite end of the passageway and then cut left; the two men were running behind her. She was afraid they might shoot her, even though she didn't know why. She had never done anything to hurt anyone. Millions of paranoid scenarios raced through her mind, almost as fast as each foot raced across the slippery ground.

Amber emerged from the alley and darted through a three lane road. A Buick and a Toyota were both forced to slam their brakes as the young woman ran across their path. The Buick honked its horn as the Toyota slammed into its rear end. Hub caps and glass flew all over the street.

As she crossed the street, there was a Burger King on her right. She ran into the Burger King and darted through the seating area and out the other side. When she came out of the restaurant, she doubled back the opposite way hoping to throw her pursuers off. She figured they would keep running right through the Burger King and on down the road.

But she was smart, even smarter than the CIA.

She kept running, zig zagging through the soggy city streets.

She had lost them. The old men couldn't keep up with her, but she was in need of some wind herself. She slowed to a walk. Her heart was thumping inside her chest the way it hadn't in years. Blood was screaming past her lungs and she could feel her heavy breathing in her ears. She was already planning how to circle back around and retrieve her backpack. She ran her hands through her blond hair, which is what she did when she was thinking.

She was safe, though, having outwitted the Feds. She lowered her guard and rounded the next corner onto the sidewalk. As she did a large man in a police uniform was standing right there. He grabbed her and said, "Gotcha, Amber." The uniformed police officer spoke into his shoulder mounted radio, "I have her, we're on the corner of 4th and Warren."

Amber tried to bite the officer, but he was quick on his toes and prepared for that. Apparently, she was not the first person he had nabbed. She screamed, yelled, and flailed in a futile attempt to get away. It was no use. She protested loudly, "I haven't done anything wrong! I'm innocent! Why are you doing this? It's not illegal to sleep in the alley."

The officer was silent, but within seconds four different police squad cars arrived and surrounded her. Out of the back of one of them she saw the overcoat from the alley. The CIA man. But as he emerged from the car, she knew he was not from the CIA. He was from her past.

The man held out his arms and said, "You need to come home Amber."

"Why?" she yelled back defiantly, as the rain ran down her face.

"It's about your brother."

"What has my self righteous, overly pious brother done now that I need to be bothered with him? He seems to get along just fine without me or my input."

"He's dead." The man's voice cracked as he announced this. "Someone shot him this morning while he was preaching at his church. Your mother and I would like you to come home, if only for a little while as we make arrangements."

Amber was stunned.

"*He lies*," the voices chimed in, attempting to plant doubt in her thoughts. She pushed the voices away, knowing that her father would not lie to her. Ignore her, maybe. Lecture her, definitely. Lie to her, never.

"Okay, Daddy."

Amber crawled into the back of the blue squad car. She was wet and cold, and numb on the inside. Her father sat beside her. Neither one of them spoke. It was an awkward silence broken only by the occasional squawk of the police car radio. Finally, Amber asked the obvious question.

"What happened?"

"Well," Amber's graying father began somberly, "Your brother was preaching at his church this morning, like he always does. You know how he loved his church. While he was preaching, a man stood up, walked to the front near the platform and shot him in the chest. He died right there on the chancel while your sister-in-law Elaine held him."

There was another long pause as Amber absorbed the information.

"I am surprised you didn't hear about it. It seems to be a pretty big story. I'm sorry that we startled you. I didn't know how to find you by myself so I called in a few favors with the police department. All I knew was that you were in the city somewhere. But Amber, you should know; the police want to talk to you."

"Why?" Amber asked solemnly.

"Honey, they have some suspicions you are somehow involved; not that you did it, but that somehow this traces back to you."

"I have not seen Adam in years. Why would they think someone shooting him would have anything to do with me?"

With that he looked her in the eyes, and for the first time since he first heard his son was dead, the man cried. Tears came out of his eyes and down his cheeks as he said, "Because, the man who killed your brother Adam, they think he was one of your friends. The police keep a close eye on you folks, and as soon as they identified him they knew he was a street person, and that he was one of your friends. It didn't take them long to start making guesses about what might have happened."

"That's ridiculous. None of my friends would do this. You're lying."

"He lies. Don't trust him. Remember why you left," affirmed the voices inside her head.

"What is his name?" she demanded.

"His name was Steve Gadara."

With that the voices laughed uncontrollably and most vilely. Their joyous celebration finished with slithering praise, "*Good job Steve, good job. Now it is your turn, Amber.*"

The young woman was no longer able to handle the information coming at her from both her father and the voices. The weight of her own emotions about Adam and Steve both being dead pounded at her soul. She grabbed her ears with her hands and doubled over in psychic pain and yelled loudly from the back of the car, "No! Stop! No! It can't be!"

Her Father struggled with what to say, and in the end said nothing. Instead his parental instinct wrapped his arms around his daughters shoulders and drew her close to him. They rode in silence back to the home Amber and Adam had grown up in. It was on the other side of town, near the church where Adam ministered.

Tears streamed down her face as the rain poured outside. Amber wept as a confused woman who had been devastated by trauma. The old man wept too. It was hard to know what exactly he was weeping about. Was he weeping over his martyred son or his prodigal daughter who might be involved? No, he wept for himself. It took the death of his son for him to realize that his daughter had been as good as dead to him for years. How had he let this happen?

His lament intensified.

Mercifully, they finally arrived.

Daddy got out of the car. He reached down to lift his daughter out of the car but before he could, a deputy interrupted. Officer Wilson said, "Sir, I know this is hard, but I have orders to bring her downtown. The detective would like to question her. Thank you for helping us apprehend her."

With those words, he shut the back door and quickly got behind the wheel and sped off. It happened so fast the distraught father didn't even have the opportunity to protest. His daughter didn't either. Her posture never changed. Through the whole moment she maintained her head in her hands weeping in the backseat.

"Will this ever end?" he asked.

Upon arriving at the police station the deputy escorted Amber through the bright fluorescent lights of the lobby and through the main offices, down a hallway and through another lobby. Eventually they arrived at a small cubicle. Amber had been arrested before so she knew the police station, but she had never been inside the work area of the station. Most of her dealings with the police were for petty issues of public indecency or drunkenness. She had never made it past the front counter or the jail cells. This, however, was a far different deal than she had ever known.

To her surprise there was no interrogation room with a double-sided mirror or any other common conventions of television. Instead, she sat in a small cubicle with a very large man behind the desk pounding away at a computer keyboard. His desk was piled high with papers and file folders. There were about three different coffee cups on his desk, each one half filled. It was as if he had begun to drink out of each of them and then forgot he already had one when he poured yet another. There were candy wrappers all over the detective's desk, along with sunflower seed shells which had been spit out into a Styrofoam cup. The detective was not a good aim, for most of his shells were all around the cup, on the desk, or the floor.

Amber sat for what must have been ten minutes just waiting for the detective to finish whatever he was working on. Finally he turned to her, smiled and said, "Miss Smith, I know it is very late," he paused and glanced at his watch and continued, "or early, as it is nearly 1:30 in the morning, but I just have a few questions to ask you. I am Detective Richard Wright and I am working on your deceased brother's case.

"Here is what we know, Miss Smith. A man named Steve Gadara purchased a handgun sometime Saturday night from a man named Ray in the warehouse district. The next time Mr. Gadara turned up was on the bus to church the next morning. From the bus stop he walked or hitchhiked to your brother's church. Once at church, he kept snooping around, asking questions about your brother until he found out where he was. Once he saw your brother, he stood up and shot him. Now, where this gets interesting, Miss Smith, is that we have two eyewitnesses who indicate the last time they saw Mr. Gadara he was with you. Apparently the two of you were drinking in the alley together. Did the two of you drink together Saturday night?"

Amber opened her mouth, but nothing came out. The way the detective delivered the narrative so matter-of-fact caught her off guard. She was still processing her brother's death. Two hours ago everything was normal; now her world had violently shattered apart and apparently someone thought she was to blame.

"Did Mr. Gadara sleep with you in the alley?"

She answered a soft and quiet, "No." Then added, "He always slept in the shelter. He liked the bunks."

"Were you romantically involved?"

Again she answered, but more emphatically, "No. We were just friends."

"Did Mr. Gadara talk about anything unusual on Saturday night that, in hindsight might have been suspicious?"

Amber thought hard. "No. We just drank together. He really didn't talk about anything. I did most of the talking, but neither one of us talked that much. We never did. I think that is why we are such good friends."

"Friends?" the detective snorted incredulously. "Are you sure you were just friends? Is it not true that you performed sexual favors for Mr. Gadara so that he would kill your brother for you?"

"What?" Amber cried.

"*Yes, you did,*" the voices lied to her.

The detective did not let up. He unleashed a barrage of questions upon her in rapid succession giving her no time to answer any of them. "Why did you want your brother dead? How long had you been planning his murder? Was it Steve's idea or yours to buy the handgun? Did you give him the money for the gun? Do you expect us to believe you had nothing to do with this at all, Amber? Do you?"

"It is all your fault, Amber. You killed Adam and Steve!" the voices screamed.

Amber sat in the office cubicle chair and cried.

Detective Wright allowed her a moment to sob, and then, as if he were a totally different person from the one who had just now attacked her with a volley of accusations, gently said, "That's okay. Take your time. It'd be better if you just told us exactly what happened."

"*Oooooh, tell him everything.*" the voices hissed.

Amber wiped her nose with her sleeve and pushed her dirty but still naturally wavy hair out of her face. Taking a deep breath she composed herself and said to the chubby detective, "I did not have anything to do with what you say I did. I do not know why Steve killed Adam." Her voice rose and she yelled, "But I hate him for it!" There was a long pause as she cried. Then she continued, "Maybe he figured out who I was, or something, I don't know. But I didn't have anything to do with it. I am guilty of a lot of things but this is not one of them. I never understood my brother, and he never understood me, but I loved him. He was a good man."

"*A dead man,*" the voices giggled.

"Now he's a dead man," the Detective said. The echo between Detective Wright and the voices was beginning to have an effect on Amber. He continued, "And I believe you killed him. I have no hard evidence, but I will get it." The interrogator popped a handful of sunflower seeds into his mouth, smiled at her again and said, "You may go, Miss Smith, but don't leave town." He turned his large, balding head back toward his computer screen and assumed the same posture he'd had when she came into his work space.

Amber rose and slowly walked out into the hallway. A uniformed police officer was waiting for her. The officer escorted her out of the maze of office space and to the main lobby. Amber's father was sitting on a hard cushioned seat waiting for her.

Neediness flooded over the young woman. She ran to her father and threw her arms around his neck. She collapsed into his fatherly grasp in a way she hadn't since she was a little girl. He took her weight and held her up, although he himself was physically and mentally exhausted too. Amber cried, and as she wept she kept repeating, "I didn't know anything about it Daddy! I didn't know anything about it Daddy!"

The middle aged man pattered her back and said reassuringly, "I know, I know." The problem was, he didn't know. Down in the pit of his stomach he was unsettled. The thought that his estranged daughter could have killed his devoted son would never have crossed his mind if he lived for a million years. However, even he had to admit the circumstantial evidence was mounting; and mounting quickly.

He suppressed that thought and led Amber out of the police station. His Volvo was parked in the well lit police precinct parking lot. He drove the two of them back home and no words passed between them. There was nothing to say. When they arrived home, her mother was waiting for them in the kitchen. She sat at the table with a mountain of used Kleenex around her. It was now 3:15 A.M. on Monday morning.

The three Smith's tried to sleep, nevertheless rest and peace were elusive. The next morning found them all awake early. Amber took a long hot shower, something she had not had in a long time; nevertheless, she was unable to enjoy it. Sometime around noon one of Adam's colleagues, Pastor Butch Gregory from a nearby community Church dropped in. Adam's wife, Elaine, had already contacted Butch about leading and planning a funeral service to be held next Sunday, exactly one week from the dreaded day. Adam had always trusted Butch, Elaine said, and right now the last thing she wanted to do was take care of all the funeral details.

The phone rang without ceasing. There were television crews outside on the lawn. The family did not have any time at all to process the events which had taken place. It was as if they were in a made-for-television movie and they were watching other people go through these actions. Grief had no avenue for expression and the fishbowl was getting worse. Larry King, Nancy Grace, and Barbara Walters all wanted exclusive interviews with the Smith's. They had turned it all down; they just wanted it all to go away.

Amber thought about running away, heading back to the streets where she was anonymous. She could find a new city to hide in. No one would ever find her.

"Yes, run," the voices counseled her. "Run to Phoenix. Run to Los Angeles. Run to Denver. Run!"

"No, I've been running my whole life. I will not run now."

"You are doomed."

She mumbled a reply of, "Maybe?"

"DIEENDITNOWMAKEITEASY!"

Amber sat in her father's home study with the curtains closed and the lights off. She pondered the easy necessity of suicide. No one would ever believe her; ever. She was smart enough to know that it did not matter what she said, the police were out to get her. This would make it impossible to go back on the streets.

Even though it had been three years since she'd last seen her brother, she missed him. Her heart hurt so badly, she did not know what to do. Maybe these voices were right. The grief was becoming unbearable.

"*Yes*," they whispered inside her head.

Amber walked across the room and turned on the lamp on her father's old desk. She sat down, reached into the top drawer and pulled out a blank sheet of white paper. With a decorative fountain pen she picked up from its mounted perch, Amber began to write:

Mom and Dad,

So sorry it ended this way. I did not do anything to hurt Adam, but no one will ever believe me and the police are after me. I don't even know if you believe me.
Years ago I ran away because I wanted to be free. Now, that freedom looks like an illusion. When Steve killed Adam, he also killed my way of life. I hate him for it. Goodbye.

Amber

She sat in the room and read the note to herself several times while running her hands through her hair. She planned to walk out the backdoor and try to sneak through the neighbors yard and avoid the media frenzy outside. Then she would catch the number seven bus to the waterfront. From there she would jump off the bridge and plummet to her death. The bridge wasn't that high, but it was high enough to get the job done. She knew that from experience; more than one friend had bought it that way.

But before she could leave, tears again formed in her eyes and they plopped down onto the paper. All Amber could think about was her brother and how, him being the big brother, taught her how to sneak into this room and play in Daddy's things. She just couldn't stop crying.

"There you are," said Elaine. Elaine was Adam's wife; Adam's widow. "We wondered where you were."

Elaine had a handful of tissue and bloodshot eyes from weeping. Her dark brown hair was pulled back in a pony tail and she wore a pair of blue jeans and a faded out sweat shirt over her tiny frame. It was obvious she had neglected her appearance; nevertheless there was an inner strength inside her which Amber immediately, and for the first time, noticed.

Elaine looked around the room and smiled. "Adam was just talking about this room a few weeks ago. Sammy had crawled into Adam's study at home and somehow ripped the "Crossing of the Red Sea" out of his study Bible. Adam told me it reminded him of when you and he used to sneak in here and play. He was very sad when he learned that your father knew all along, but wanted you guys to think you were getting away with something."

With that thought a light giggle broke over Elaine's face, but the thought of children and a family just made Amber cry more. The isolation she felt, the ridiculous life she had lived, it was all punctuated by how happy her brother had been.

"Miserable," they whispered. "You are pathetic."

In a furtive moment, Elaine glanced down to the desk and quickly took in the suicide note. Elaine didn't respond immediately. She picked up the note and sat down across from Amber on a straight back chair. She read over it again. Amber continued to weep, aware that her sister-in-law had discovered her intentions.

Finally, Elaine said, "I believe you. Does that count for anything?"

Amber asked, "Really? Or are you just saying that because you feel sorry for me?"

"I don't feel sorry for anyone, right now. Amber, yesterday a crazy man shot and killed my husband in front me, my children and all my friends. In an instant, my life was changed, forever. I do not have enough emotion in me right now to feel sorry for anyone. But I know you didn't have anything to do with it. There is no way you would or could. It's not in you. You are a kind person. I do not know what connection this Steve man had with you, but down deep inside of me I just know you didn't have anything to do with it. I know you are innocent. It might be that God is telling me this."

"What does God have to do with any of this?" Amber asked, almost angrily.

"Everything," the widow replied. "God has everything to do with everything."

"Did God kill my brother, then?"

"YESYESYESYESYESYESYES! God killed your brother and Steve," the voices insisted. "It is his fault. Blame him, not us."

"No," Elaine answered, but as she did she wept again. She shook her head back and forth as she pulled out tissue from her sweatshirt pocket. "No, God didn't kill Adam. A crazy man did. I will never hold God responsible for what people do. The Lord instead helps us work through this life as a preparation for the next. Your brother, my husband, died doing what he loved to do. There was nothing that thrilled him more than telling people about how much Jesus loves them. He'd dedicated his life to doing this. That he died doing it, at such an early age, is hard to swallow, but his life had meaning and purpose."

"I don't understand. Meaning and purpose sound like so much gobbledy goop."

"That is because," Elaine paused, "because you do not know the Jesus who Adam and I have loved and served. If you knew him, then you would understand. Everybody dies, and those who die with Jesus have no fear of anything because love overcomes all fear. I know Adam. I know he was disappointed at dying, because he had big plans for Mosaic Church. He always wanted to do an archaeology dig in the Holy Land and he had that book he never finished. None of that will ever happen now. But the important things, he was at peace with."

With those words, Elaine felt the prompting of the Holy Spirit deep within her. It was so subtle it surprised her because she had been spiritually numb for the last twenty-four hours. But she had learned to obey the promptings of the Holy Spirit through the years of hard ministry. She looked at Amber and asked, "Honey, would you like to have the same peace Adam had, and that I have? You don't have to be afraid of the Devil anymore. It's easy to do, you should know it means changing the way you think and live. It means committing your life to Christ. Do you want to?"

"It is a trick. She lies."

Miraculously, Amber nodded her head yes. She blotted out the voices in her mind. She was unable to speak because the emotions of the moment swelled around her. Elaine took her hand and said to her, "If you mean it, then pray what I pray. Dear God, please forgive me of my mistakes, of my sins."

"NONONONONONONOYOUAREMINEYOUAREOURS!" The voices screeched opposition to Amber's new course of action. They were, though, powerless to stop her.

Amber repeated the line. It had been a long time since she had prayed. She paused at the word "sins," and thought about all the things she had done that she knew were wrong. Then she said, "sins" with a strong clear voice.

A demonic wail bellowed inside her soul. Amber felt years of spiritual oppression lift off her soul.

Elaine continued, "Jesus, I believe you are who the Bible says you are, and I invite you into my heart." Amber repeated the lines and as she did a smile formed on her face, but the smile had begun forming in her heart.

"I commit my life to you. Amen." From that moment on, for the rest of her life, Amber never heard the voices again.

The women ended the prayer and hugged. A feeling of emotion, Elaine called it confirmation, filled the room. Amber felt free and alive. The first thing she did was wad the suicide note up and throw it away. Her life was better now; it was going to be better now. She had something to live for.

They walked into the kitchen where Amber's mother was talking on the phone. As Elaine and Amber walked in, Mommy hung up and looked at the two women. It wasn't a smile, but a settled look of relief washed over her face.

"That was Detective Wright from the police," Amber's and Adam's mother began. "He told me they found a note at the church which they had missed yesterday. It was written on a church bulletin. It was from," her voice quivered, "that man who killed our Adam. In the note he wrote that it was voices inside him that told him to do it. The note said he didn't want to do it but that the voices were making him and he was sorry. The detective said their investigation of Steve Gadara indicates he had spent time under the care of a psychologist for mental health issues. That is why he'd run away and lived on the streets."

The aging mother paused, and then looked at her only living child. "To make a long story short, Amber, the police are dropping you as a suspect. They no longer believe you had anything to do with it. Of course, we knew that all along."

Elaine pondered in her heart the last thing her husband had said before he died. He had asked the question, "Why?" At the time, it seemed like a desperate cry for understanding in the heat of tragedy. But right now, she perceived that maybe he was asking, "Why?" in a different way. Maybe he meant, "I wonder why this has happened? Or perhaps, I wonder what God will do with this ugly moment to turn it into something beautiful?"

"Why?" was his question. Perhaps an answer is, "Amber."

Legacy:
A Hyperbolic Parody Parable of Stereotypes

In the year 2409 the last identifiable group of Baptists left earth. The worldwide laws which criminalized preaching against social sin made the previously marginalized radical religious group outlaws. Seeking a place to practice their faith in peace with religious liberty, the group secured a multi-phase, multi-platform space vessel. The name of this vessel was Smith and Helwys. *Mars had already been colonized as well as two of the moons around Jupiter. Therefore, the breakaway group planned to leave this solar system altogether and find an inhabitable planet in a nearby star system. When they left earth, they had a total compliment of 1,440 people. These were mostly family units as well as some senior adults. There was great discussion about the senior adults, but since they had funded the mission it was decided to let them come. The leader of this group was called "Paster." The 1,440 were divided into smaller groups called "departments." Each of the departments had a department leader called a "deecun." Most activity on board the vessel was organized by departments. This included job assignments, sleeping, potlucking, and worship. There were seven departments on the* Smith and Helwys. *After the department division, there was a smaller divisional unit called "Sundy Skul." Each Sundy Skul was led by a team leader called a "quarterly" Sundy Skuls were mandated by ship constitution to meet before worship on the Church Deck on NFLday, the first day in the seven-day weekly cycle. The Sundy Skul also met Wednesdy evenings for prayer.*

For two years this system worked. Then the unthinkable happened.

Scotte ate his potluck with eyes full of sleep. He had been arguing again with his wife, Stacy. The argument was the same one they had been having since the *Smith and Helwys* broke earth orbit. She did not like their Sundy Skul quarterly. He was dull and boring. For nine months they had been studying the beast from the apocalyptic books Daniel and Revelation. Their quarterly's name was Hal. Hal was fascinated by the Beast and prophecy and had kept showing the Sundy Skul files and files of old fashioned Powerpoint slides illustrating who the beast might be.

Hal believed it was Pope Mary Theresa II back on earth because she had instigated a planet wide one child per couple decree. Most in the Sundy Skul believed it was not Pope Mary Theresa II but was the new computer brain which came on-line five years ago. The computer brain was on a satellite in low earth orbit. The brain was built originally to control earth's climate; particularly to warm up the globe since the two decades of global cooling had significantly decreased animal life in the northern hemisphere. Plummeting temperatures had been to blame for the epidemic of feline cholera that reduced the cat population to only ten percent of what it was in its heyday back in the late 22nd century.

However, once the brain came on-line it had increasingly become a tool of the UNITEDNATIONS. They kept using its spreading array of sensors to monitor groups they viewed as subversive. Number one on this group were the Baptists. A close second was the Teamsters Union.

As he chewed his potluck eggs and biscuits Scotte hashed out his wife's complaint. Stacy had said, "I don't care who the beast is. I'm just bored with it. It's not that I don't believe there is a beast; it just doesn't matter any more. He's been on this topic longer than I carried either one of our children. It just seems to me that Hal is going to keep at it until he convinces us it is the Pope. I'm just tired of it." Stacy wanted her and Scotte to petition the departmental deecun for a Sundy Skul transfer.

Specifically, she wanted to transfer to her sister's Sundy Skul. Her sister Barbara was always telling her all the wonderful things her group was doing. They would stargaze together off the port bow, potluck ethnic foods and swap recipes, as well as play movies together. Scotte and Stacy's Sundy Skul never did any of that.

The problem Scotte was having is that the Sundy Skul was assigned, by lot, when they boarded the ship. No one had ever asked for a transfer before. Sure, some of the people who worked in his engineering department had talked about switching, but never seriously. Stacy just did not understand how this might disrupt the stability of life aboard the *Smith and Helwys*. Scotte did not know what to do.

Just as he finished his juice and was about to leave Fellowshiphall and go to work, his watch went off. The crystal clear image of his wife Stacy appeared on the screen and she said, "I love you honey. I am sorry we fought. Please forgive me, its not that big a deal. I guess I'm just cranky. That's all."

"Me too, honey," said Scotte. "Tonight, when I get home let us pray about it and see what Jesus wants us to do? When will you be home from ballet?"

"About six. The kids are with your mom. Love you. Have a great day."

"You too," the young engineer said as he smiled. He had a great wife. She was talented too. When she left earth she gave up a promising career with the very prestigious San Francisco Straight Ballet. As life on board the *Smith and Helwys* settled down she had used her dancing talent to instruct. She had about forty-five students ranging in ages from children to seniors.

Scotte walked out of Fellowshiphall on the Potluck Deck and down the auxillary concourse, caught a hotairlift and made his way to the Engineering Room. The *Smith and Helwys* was a multi-phased vessel which meant it had multiple engineering stations; one for each of its four phases. The ship could split into two, three, or even four different vessels. When the ship was unified, the engine room looked like one large room with four different work stations.

This design was used by science teams exploring strange new worlds. The different phases of the main vessel could detach and operate independently for indefinite amounts of time. Then they could reattach for the long journey back to earth or simply so the crew and scientists could collaborate. Each of the four phases of the ship could operate independently without the other three. When combined, the four engine phases made the ship much bigger.

When the four phases were together each independent engine connected with the other three forming a great four chambered engine much faster and efficient than any one engine could be on its own. Scotte was the second in command in the engine room and led the "Mark" engine. Shortly after takeoff the engineering crew had renamed the engines which were blandly labeled Engine "A", Engine "B", Engine "C", and Engine "D." They had decided to honor the four evangelists of the New Testament so now there was a "Matthew," "Mark," "Luke," and "John" engine. The engineers who maintained the engines were called "Ministers" and Scotte was the lead minister for Mark Engine. His only supervisor was the Senior Minister, a man named Sy Dort. As Chief Minister, Dort was the third in command on the *Smith and Helwys*, behind only the Paster and B. E. Trendy. B. E. Trendy was the Senior Minister of Ushering. His duties were to supervise the whole crew in maintaining a proper focus on their vision statements.

Trendy and Dort often had different opinions about how things should go. Dort's passion was to know the rules and then do what the rules say. Trendy was far more relational and was interested in easygoing life together. Paster often had to referee big disagreements. Because of the close knit relationships within the ship's crew, these disagreements often spilled over into the rest of the ship.

But Paster was there to keep things under control.

Several weeks later, Scotte finally had been convinced by his wife that it was time for a change. He talked to his Deecun. Unfortunately, the Deecun would only consider the request if his minister agreed. Scotte's minister was Dort.

This was not an unusual prerequisite by the Deecun. On the *Smith and Helwys*, all discussions, whether work related or spiritually related, were interwoven into the same command structure. Therefore, it would be up to Dort to grant or deny the Sundy Skul change request.

Scotte's duty shift was over, but he didn't go home. He climbed up the metal spiral stairwell surrounding the four-chambered engine up to the observation deck. He walked across the transparent floor and entered Dort's platform. The middle-aged man was sitting at his desk with his Bible opened.

"A word sir?" Scotte asked meekly.

"Sure, Scotte. What can I do for you?"

"Well, my wife and I have been praying about it, sir, and, well, something is missing from our lives. We think it might be helpful if we made some changes to the way we do things. So, well, here, sir." As he said the word "here" Scotte slipped a written request signed by him and his wife across the mahogany desk. "I think this explains everything. I'm not a man of many words."

Dort's long face beheld the letter and he read it quickly. "What? Why? This doesn't make any sense to me? Your position in that class was predestined; that is where you are supposed to be. I don't know, Scotte."

The young man could tell by his boss' demeanor that his request would be denied. Scotte was about to apologize and turn to leave when the room jerked and began to shake violently. Red lights began to flash and the emergency siren screeched. Neither Dort nor Scotte had ever experienced this before. It was a completely new sensation neither were prepared for.

Something was wrong. The *Smith and Helwys* was in some kind of danger. Dort shouted to Scotte, "Go lock down the Mark engine, and tell the other ministers to lock theirs down too. Scotte, make sure you vent the ion shafts."

Scotte knew what that meant. The four engines vented ion particles which were highly toxic. These particles were vented from each individual engine through four separate shafts that traversed the ship. This exhaust system worked flawlessly at getting the harmful bi-product of the engines out into space. Yet Dort and Scotte both knew that if the ship were to sustain damage and these particles escaped into the living quarters many people could get sick. Many more could die.

"Amen," said Scotte to Dort, as the two exchanged a knowing look. In a whirling instant their discussion over Sundy Skul didn't seem to matter that much.

As the engineer ran out of Dort's office, a heavy metal beam cut loose from its ceiling mount and collapsed within inches of his feet. The heavy titanium plank smashed through the clear decking and shattered the walkway. He was trapped on the wrong side of the emerging chasm and was still at least twenty feet away from the stairway.

The adrenaline rushed inside his frightened body. Somehow he had to get down to the lower deck and lock down the engines. He whispered a prayer, "Lord Jesus Christ, Son of God, have mercy upon my Baptist soul," and with a whoosh he jumped on the titanium beam that had smashed the deck. He landed on it in such a way that he straddled it, facing down toward the lower deck. He could see clearly the activity below him as he hovered between the upper administrative level and the floor below.

He spotted his colleague, an able hermeneut named Haddon who was the team leader for the Matthew engine. Scotte yelled down to him, "Minister says to lock down all four gospels until we figure out what happened. Tell the others."

"Amen," shouted Haddon as he ran off to the other side of the engine room.

Now all Scotte had to do was to find a way to vent the ion shaft before a rupture occurred. Scotte thought to himself, "If another beam like this collapses anywhere near that shaft, it's a safe bet there will be many funerals to come." Scotte hated funerals, especially long Baptist funerals, so he decided to do everything he could to keep that from happening.

He was still a long way away from the shaft, though, and still suspended in midair. With a lurch, the beam he straddled continued its slow rumble toward the steel deck below. The thirty foot drop would probably break his leg. That wasn't the real problem, though. The seventy ton beam and subsequent collision would certainly kill him. He had to get off.

"On Christ the solid rock I stand," sang Scotte as he quickly stood on the beam. Walking up the beam, he spotted wire meshing which had become exposed in the collapse of the Plexiglas decking above. On a leap of faith, he launched out and grabbed the meshing. It was a pirouette that would have made his wife proud.

He hung there for a moment, but gradually the meshing pulled loose like unraveling fabric. As he fell, he caught a break and smashed into what was left of the stairwell he had so casually climbed fifteen minutes earlier.

Blood began to spurt out of his forehead. Apparently he had gashed himself on the metal. Nevertheless, he was alive. Slowly, but purposefully, he navigated himself down to the floor below.

Once he was down, he ran through the corridor and quickly popped open the control panel for the shaft. All he would have to do to vent the toxic ion particles is key in the sequence code for the four engines. He keyed in Matthew's code, 28:18,19,20. That followed with the Mark engine code of 13:10 and then Luke's 13:5. Just before he entered the John engine key code, 3:16, the lights blinked off and the panel lost power.

Scotte yelped.

Just as he did, he heard Paster calling his name.

"Scotte, vent the shaft."

"I can't Paster. The power just blinked off. We'll have to do it manually."

"That is what I was afraid of," said the older man. He too was bleeding, but his wound was on his chest. There was also a splattering of blood in his grey hair.

Scotte looked at his paster and asked, "What happened, why are we falling apart? Why did this happen to us?"

Just as he asked the question, more and different types of sirens again began to blare. Paster yelled back at his man, "I don't really know what hit us. We were cruising along and suddenly we hit some sort of change in the actual physics of the space around us. It was as if in an instant all the rules of how the ship moved and functioned didn't work anymore. Scotte, it felt like a vortex of swirling, constant change opened up within the vacuum of space. All of our instruments kept showing constant variations both outside and inside the ship. The changes were occurring so quickly once we adjusted to match, it changed again. I ordered us to reverse course and when I did, the ship buckled and pressure from the outside began to collapse the outer hull.

"And Scotte, we're still not out of it. I left Trendy in charge on the main pulpit, because I didn't know what had happened down here. The ship is in disarray. None of the hotairlifts are working, and the Missions Deck is inoperable. I had to crawl through the ventilation ducts to get here."

Paster then looked around, as if looking for someone, and then asked, "Where is Dort?"

"He is stuck on the upper administrative deck, on his platform. I think he's okay, but there is probably no way he can get down here. We better hurry, Brother."

"Amen," agreed Paster.

Scotte knelt down and opened the service hatch directly below the panel. Scotte crawled in first, then Paster followed. About twenty or twenty-five feet later they were in a small room directly below the four engines where the ion exhaust flowed into the long shaft which opened up into space.

The valve had never moved manually. The two men pushed on it together, but it wouldn't budge. Scotte prayed aloud, "We can do all things through the one who gives us strength." He kept repeating that over and over. "We can do all things through the one who gives us strength. We can do all things through the one who gives us strength." Paster began to pray it as well. Suddenly, the valve budged. Both men let out a cheer. As they gave the wheel its first half turn, a rivet on the shaft popped and shot across the small room like a bullet. Red toxins spewed out and hit Paster directly in the face.

Scotte yelled, "Paster!"

"Keep pushing," Paster ordered as he gasped and choked.

They did, and finally the valve turned and a whoosh of air passed through and the sucking sound of space filled their ears.

The last thing Scotte saw before he blacked out was his paster lying on the deck.

Paster died within five minutes of his intense exposure to the dangerous ions. Fortunately for Scotte, most of those particles escaped out into space before they saturated the chamber he was in. He only suffered minor lung damage. The Balm of Gilead station had given him a mild antihistamine to fix the symptoms. It would be a while, though, before he would be feeling normal.

Miraculously, there were only two other fatalities onboard the *Smith and Helwys*. One was a little baby who was only weeks old and the other was an older man who fell in the initial lurch and broke his neck. It was the death of Paster, however, that caused fear and doubt to spread throughout the crew.

Paster had been the one who organized the mission in the beginning. He often talked in the NFLday sermons how he believed God had called him to lead the persecuted Baptists out into a brave new world, to go boldly where no Baptist had gone before. He was the spiritual leader of the self-exiled refugees.

Unfortunately, there was precious little time to mourn the past or the dead. The *Smith and Helwys* was still in the tempest of change; although the immediate threat had abated. Once Dort was freed from the administrative center above the four gospels, he and Trendy held an emergency meeting of the Ship Council. The Ship Council was the main decision making group for the *Smith and Helwys*. It comprised the Paster, the six ministers, (Dort, Trendy, and the four team leaders for the engines), the seven deecuns, and one at-large minister elected from the ship's crew for a total of fifteen.

Under normal circumstances, the Ship Council met monthly to discuss and decide on the ongoing affairs of the ship. They usually met in a conference room called The Upper Room. Each one had a well appointed chair at a rounded conference table. Holographic displays were in front of each chair for ready access to documents and data. Miraculously, none of the elements of this room had been damaged in the crisis. The lack of damage provided a bit of insulation from just how precarious their situation was.

There was one looming absence at the table, however. Paster's chair was empty. They spent a few moments in prayer and reflected from Psalm Twenty-three—"The Lord is our Paster," one of them had said. Then the Council talked about a new leader.

Deecun Isaac Car said, "I think B. E. Trendy should lead us now and become our Paster. He is the one Paster put in charge on the Main Pulpit when he went down to engineering. I think he understands our times and knows what we should do. It seems logical to me."

"I agree," said Minister Willow. Willow was the only female minister and she was the team leader for the Luke Engine. "Minister Trendy has the kind of personality and people skills to move us through this present crisis. The people trust him, and we need his calm and gentle leadership."

"Hold on a minute," said Minister Haddon. "I personally think Dort is God's man for the moment. B. E. Trendy is a great guy and wonderful minister with good ideas, but what we need now is intricate expertise in how the engines work and the engineering of the *Smith and Helwys*. We do not need people skills now. We need intellect and orthodoxy of mechanics. Sy Dort is the right man for right now. We do not need persuasion and personality. We need strength and conviction."

Several others piped up and the discussion became very sectarian. The council was almost equally divided down the middle. Three deecuns were in favor of Trendy, four were for Dort. Amongst the ministers, only Willow went with Trendy outright. Two others, Haddon and a very large man named Criswell, favored Dort. The at-large minister, a curious but inconsistent man named Fosdick, voted for Trendy. This made the count six to five in favor of Dort. It came down to Scotte's vote.

Scotte, however, faced a dilemma. It had only been six short hours since he'd stood on Dort's platform requesting a Sundy Skul transfer. He thought about how dismissive he'd been of his request and the near contempt for the thought of any kind of change. Could a man like that really lead a whole ship full of people? Could Dort be the new paster? He knew Paster, the now dead Paster, would never have responded that way to his emotional needs.

At the same time he believed no one knew the ship better than Dort. Sy Dort was a mechanical genius who knew the four gospels better than anyone. He could not choose at this time. He was textbook undecided.

The inability to make a clear choice afforded a chance for peace. Trendy addressed the group. "I suggest that for the time being, Sy and I share duties and work as a team. After we get the *Smith and Helwys* stabilized we will come back to this issue and think about it some more. Right now all that matters is that we are on the same team."

Dort nodded agreement, but did not say anything. Everyone else agreed with Trendy's wise words.

The next hour was spent discussing the situation the ship was in. The four ministers of the gospel reported that the engines were operating, but inexplicably operating at only seventy percent of capacity. "We seem to have hit an efficiency plateau. The ship has plateaued."

The ministers were hesitant to fire the thrusters, and their measurements were based on guesses. They didn't know what might happen if they tried to move the vessel. Haddon said he and his committee had analyzed the data and discovered something significant.

He tapped a blue button and the holographic image of the ship's four engines and their flashing red damaged sections blinked out. It was replaced by a green hued timeline of events. Haddon pointed out that the trauma to the *Smith and Helwys* occurred only after Paster ordered the ship in reverse. Going backward did damage to the drive mechanism. He reported they didn't quite know what that damage was because they could not detect it with their equipment. Nevertheless, something was wrong.

Fosdick asked, "What is our present situation. Are we moving backward, forward, or motionless?"

Scotte chimed in and answered, "We are drifting, inexplicably, forward."

"Why do you say, inexplicably forward?" asked Trendy.

Scotte gasped for air and began to wheeze. His lungs were burning and he couldn't get enough breath to speak. Everyone in the room instantly remembered that he was near death not that long ago.

Criswell answered for him. "What Scotte is referring to is the sequence of actions. The last thrust of the engine was reverse. Then, when the ship began to buckle under the emerging change he ordered a full stop. The ship should, in theory, be at a full stop or at least going backwards. But it is not. It is listing forward."

"Could it be God?" It was the first thing Dort had said since the meeting began. The rest of the Ship Council glanced at him with puzzled looks. Sensing their confusion, Dort explained, "It might be that God has brought this change to teach us dependence upon him. We are moving forward, albeit it ever so slowly, and that could be evidence of a divine thrust. I mean, God is pushing us forward and holding us together in spite of the change. He is doing it all to his glory."

"Minister," Willow asked, "are you suggesting God caused the ship to buckle?"

"No," said Dort. "I am suggesting that some evil, perhaps the Devil himself, caused the change around us but God has allowed it in order to strengthen us in the face of adversity. We must fight the change surrounding the ship and God will bring us out in his good time. This is a spiritual issue of faithfulness. God will not give us a new home until we show our faithfulness to fight the change and stay the course."

Trendy looked suspicious, and simply muttered, "I don't think so." Other than that, however, he held his thoughts to himself.

"Practically," Willow chimed in, "that really is irrelevant. What we have to do is keep working at the gospels until we are able to figure out what is going on. We have to figure out how to make them work the way they should. Our first priority must be propulsion."

"Amen," said Trendy and Dort both at the same time in a rare moment of agreement. The others around the table likewise added a loud, "Amen."

"Brethren," said the Chairman of the Deecuns, "The people are not in a good way. Every department is in chaos." These words signaled a shift in the meeting's topic for discussion.

The Chairman of the Deecuns was a portly man named Stephen. In the past, Stephen had wielded a lot of power with Paster. They often prayed together and met to discuss the wellbeing of the *Smith and Helwys'* crew and families. It was well known that Stephen's best friend was Sy Dort.

Stephen tapped his blue button in front of his chair and a ship schematic of the *Smith and Helwys* appeared floating over the table. It was easy to tell that the ship was in bad shape. Most of the hologram was flashing red.

"The Missions Department is completely inoperable," he said as he began the details of his report. "The Potluck Department is operational, we are able to eat. However, we are only at sixty percent service capacity. The only department that seems to be somewhat okay is the Prayer Department. Which is good," he continued somberly, "because everybody is in prayer."

"Medically, we are fine for the moment. The Balm of Gilead has reported to me there doesn't seem to be anything about the change storm adversely affecting the human body. It only affected the ship. There is a high level of panic, though, throughout the *Smith and Helwys*. This panic has led many to wonder about the crisis of leadership we are currently facing. Some people have openly suggested that we go back to the world. One man, I will not say who it is, told me, 'It might be tough and crazy back on earth, but at least we know what we are dealing with. There are too many unknowns about the changes we might encounter in space. We have no blueprint for how to do this. It was foolish to leave.'

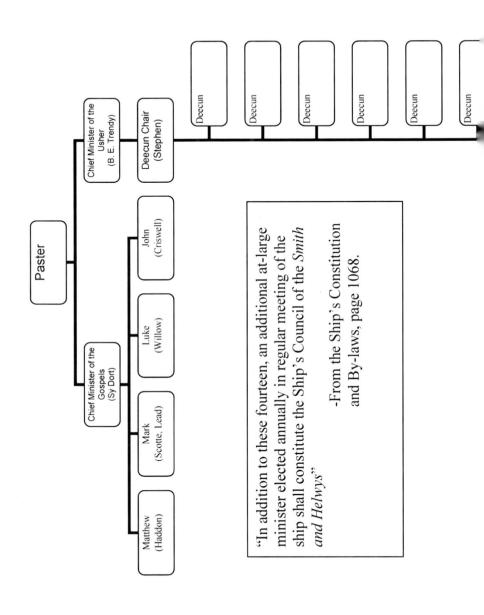

"I prayed with him and told him to calm down, but I think there are many Baptists who feel this way right now. I cannot emphasize how important it is that we have strong leadership right now to get us decisively through this change."

With that, three or four of the other Ship Council replied, "Amen!" It was clear to all this line was a not-too-subtle endorsement for Dort as the new Paster.

Deecun Stephen continued. "I have assigned teams to clean-up duty. We should have most of the good ship accessible within three days. Until then, we ask everyone to make do. Crews have begun repairing the structural damages; the main one of course being that giant beam which plowed through engineering. We don't know how long those repairs will take. What we do know is we can function as is indefinitely."

He tapped a red button and closed his data screen as he wound down his report. "One more thing," he said. "In two days we will have a ship wide memorial service for the three who died in the incident, including Paster. I know you will all be there."

"Amen," they all said.

The funeral was held on the Church Deck. There were many tearful testimonies to all three of those who had died and much moving music. Since Paster was not there to give the eulogy and neither Trendy nor Dort had been officially elected to any new position, it was agreed upon that the eulogy should be given by Paster Sandi Creak. Sandi was one of the oldest travelers on the *Smith and Helwys*. She had no official function on the vessel, but was one of the most respected pilgrims. She had survived both the horrific persecution of Christians that had occurred in the Southeastern part of North Amerika in her early ministry. Years later, in a completely separate wave of persecution, she was part of the forced exile of Pasters out of Europe when she was well into her 70's. It was this later event which pushed her to join the *Smith and Helwys* on its journey for a new home as Paster Emeritus. Sandi was often emotional and energetic in her deliveries, but age had taken its toll.

As she climbed upon the Church Pulpit, she opened her ancient translation of the Bible. Most of the Baptists used the new SIV—the Space Intergalactic Version. Sandi, however, clung to the old time religion and used a Bible handed down through the years by her family. It was called an NIV—New International Version. The teens onboard always giggled when Paster Sandi brought the sermon from her old fashioned "New" version.

But no one was giggling today. Her experience and wisdom were greatly needed and appreciated. Deecun Stephen helped her take her place on the Church Pulpit. Sandi slowly opened her Bible and began to speak.

"*Just as man is destined to die once, and after that to face judgment.* Those words, from Hebrews 9:27 remind us that death comes for all of us at some point or another. What really matters is whether we are prepared for the evaluation—the Bible calls it judgment—of our souls that will occur after death.

For the little baby that has perished we trust the love of God to protect her. She never knew the heartache of life, but instead is living in eternity. For our brother Hutchinson who died when he fell, we know he believed. I knew him well, since he was my age. We often prayed together. He is with Jesus now.

As for our Paster, Oh dear Paster," she began to weep as she said the word, "Paster." "We know that he was a good man who served God with all he had. He was most Jesus-like all the time, but never more so than when he gave his very life to save ours.

"We grieve today for his wife and children. May the Sacred Spirit comfort them all and draw them close to the Lord.

"But for us, we have to keep this one thing in mind. Since we left home we have faced very few trials. But today, our leader is dead. Moses is dead on Nebo, Saul is dead on Gilboa," her voice rose in tenacity and volume with these phrases, "and Josiah has died in battle. Like the ancient Hebrews of old, we must decide one vital question. What now shall we do?

"In the future, many years from now, decades or even perhaps centuries from now," her voice slowed and she almost whispered, "men and women will talk about this time period in history, in Christian history, in Baptist history" her voice now rising and reaching a crescendo, "as the time when in a great moment of crisis important things happened and decisions were made that mattered." She paused her sermon and looked intently out across the nearly 1,437 of them. "Brothers and sisters, dry your tears and warm your hearts. It is time for us to embrace our legacy."

With that last line she closed her well worn Bible and stepped down from the Church Pulpit and took her seat. A sense of solemnity and consecration swept over the *Smith and Helwys*. Intuitively in their hearts everyone knew that Paster Sandi had been correct in her analysis. They were in the middle of a watershed. The change storm outside the ship and the emotional trauma inside the vessel had created an epoch making moment. This moment would determine their future and the future of their group for generations to come.

Not only had their leader died, but something had altered the physics of their universe. Things were not working as they once did. It was more than a paradigm shift, it was a universal shift in reality. The way they responded to these changes in leadership and in worldview would define who they would become.

The service was nearing a close. The whole ship stood and sang, "Amazing Grace, How Sweet the Sound." As Scotte stood next to his wife, he thought about the ominous nature of the words to that song. The *Smith and Helwys* was indeed in "many danger, toils, and snares." The storm had come upon them quickly and caused great distress. But the ancient song wrote about dangers and snares in the past tense. As he sang, he affirmed his faith in the Lord God and prayed silently, "May we someday sing about coming through this present darkness."

There was a stirring in his heart of hope when the familiar refrain, "was blind but now I see" echoed through the entire deck. That was the perfect description for him and his engineers. They thought they had vision to see how the four gospels were running, but obviously they were blind to something about them. It was their blindness that caused the dramatic drop off in efficiency. It was also their blindness to know why they were only listing along instead of purring through space.

He was also blind as to why the ship could not go in reverse. As an engineer the conundrum made no sense. He tried to quiet these thoughts, though, and finish the song. The congregation spontaneously reached across their pews and began to hold hands as they rapturously sang the last stanza. It was a sign of unity and strength and smiles broke out on many sad faces as they resonated:

> *"When we've been there, ten thousand years.*
> *Bright shining as the sun.*
> *We've no less days to sing God's praise,*
> *than when we first begun."*

The celestial song and Paster Sandi Creak's sermon both brought a harmonious feeling of hope and unity in the midst of great pain and difficulty. Such is the glory of Christian worship.

The funeral concluded and most of the people filed into the Potluck Deck for the Funeral Potluck. Scotte, however, made his way to the front of the Church Deck near the Church Pulpit. He stood over the body of his Paster and wept. The words of an old poem came to his mind. He couldn't remember who wrote it or when, but the words seemed to fit the moment. He cried out, "O Paster! my Paster! our fearful trip is done."

He stood there for several minutes before he realized Dort and Trendy were also there. Both men had come up alongside him. Trendy put his hand on Scotte's shoulder and said, "You were with him when he died. That must be hard for you. I want you to know, Scotte, you are in my prayers. If you want to talk about it, I'll always be available."

"Thank you," Scotte said. "When the bolt burst, he knew if he didn't let go of the valve he would die. But he held on anyway. He didn't let go. He yelled at me to keep at it, even though I wanted to stop and help him. He was so brave."

"You were brave too," B. E. Trendy offered. "In all this discussion it has been lost exactly how much you did to save the *Smith and Helwys*. Thank you, for your bravery and courage."

"Amen," said Dort, "I fully agree. We must learn what God wants to teach us right now in these difficult days. More bravery will be needed in the future. I will pray that you find and discover the lesson God wants you, and us, to learn. It is an honor to serve the Lord with you."

It was a holy moment as the three ministers stood over the body of their fallen Paster and wept.

Soon, though, the moment ended. It had to. The seven Deecuns moved the bodies into the cryogenic chamber. The cryogenic chamber was built into the ship to store dead bodies for safe keeping until the exiled band reached a new home. The plan was to bury the corpses in a "New Nashville" as one of their first acts. Fittingly, that plan had been Paster's plan, and now he was among the first to be preserved.

The next few days and weeks were spent repairing the *Smith and Helwys*. There was not much time for grieving or reflection as there was far too much work to do. Most all the crew was on seventeen hour shifts. There was a three day period when Scotte did not sleep at all. He even worked through NFLday. The John engine had completely died. All the engineering crews and ministers abandoned their other gospels and tried to solve the problem. Eventually, John came back on-line but no one knew why. It seemed to mystically blink off and on all by itself.

Fortunately, no more structural damage occurred to the vessel. It seemed they were safe as long as they did not attempt to fire up the thrusters. The question on all the people's minds was, "How long would the ship continue to drift in limbo?" They would never reach a new home in their current condition, regardless of how safe they were. It was apparent that eventually something bold would have to be done or they would be doomed to an eternal existence in the vacuum of space.

Six months later, Scotte and Willow sat in the Minister's Study and contemplated conspiracy. The *Smith and Helwys* was in the exact same condition with only the cosmetic repairs having been made. Nothing had changed about their inability to deal with the change vortex.

The Minister's Study was a semi-private room where the Ministers of the Gospels could read, talk, or brainstorm engineering problems. The general crew did not have access. It was located just off the main refectory of the Potluck Deck. The seven Deecuns had a similar place located on the opposite side of the Potluck Deck. It was called the Deecun's Calling.

Willow and Scotte had been analyzing the data from those crucial moments when the ship buckled and led to Paster's death. The ship seemed to pass through a vortex. The vortex was filled with high energy paradigms and volatile change matrices. The reason the ship had buckled is that the vortex sealed the moment they entered. When Paster ordered a reversal of course, the ship slammed into the sealed vortex window. It was like a bird flying into a closed glass window. From the perspective of the ship, it looked as if there was space back there, but it was shut. They could only see regular space; they were not able to achieve normal space. They were blocked.

Haddon and Criswell, the other two ministers, had seen the same data. They recommended an attempt to break the "glass" vortex window and get back into real space where life was more familiar. Both Willow and Scotte were skeptical of that plan. It might destroy the ship, plus there was no way of knowing what kind of negative side effects such a regression might have on the people on board. Willow had pushed the metaphor by saying, "shattered glass often cuts those who jump through it."

The four ministers had presented this information to the Ship Council. As had become so common of late, the group was divided. Despite the calls for harmony after Paster's death, no new leader had been elected and division had marred every meeting. Scotte felt partly responsible, since he had been unable to stand up to Dort earlier. Dort had opted for the "breaking the glass" model. He argued passionately that it was important to get back to the way things used to be. "Normalcy must be achieved," he kept repeating as he broke into a rather elegant sermon on how God had predestined this crisis to demonstrate to the crew how vital the old ways were.

Trendy, on the other hand, was hesitant. He had embraced a wave of thought permeating through certain quarters of the *Smith and Helwys*. Trendy had come to believe that the change was good. This philosophy found the change wave as the direction they should travel which would lead them to their new home.

Trendy had been successful at keeping the "breaking glass" plan from being attempted. He did not want to go back. He wanted to embrace the change. The problem for Trendy and the others who opposed the "breaking glass" plan was that there was not a suitable alternative plan.

Until now.

Willow and Scotte had devised a plan to fire all four engines at once at full throttle. The combined power of all four gospels should propel the *Smith and Helwys* forward into the change and through the forward matrix of the third wave and into the direction of progress. They would, in essence, catch the change wave and ride it out at full blast.

Neither engineer, though, knew how this 'what if' might affect the ship. It could have the same calamitous results that Paster's reversal had. There could be another glass barrier emerging just in front of them What if space-time changed again? How would the ship handle multiple changes in a small period of time? They had survived the last problem, would they survive this one? The shifts and changes might be infinite.

Answers to those questions and problems eluded them. But their core values told them, as engineers, that going forward is easier than going backward, and progress is always better than regress. The two ministers had spent no small amount of time searching the Scriptures to see if any direction for their mechanical problems could be found. Not surprisingly, it had. Their study informed them that rarely in the Bible did anyone ever go backward. Faith required forward steps into the "things hoped for" and knowledge of things "unseen." They could not see what was ahead of them, but knew it would have to be from God. If God was in this at all, he must be beckoning them forward.

They had told neither Haddon nor Criswell about their plan to emerge through the change. It was in this moment that conspiracy was birthed. They decided to by-pass the prescribed protocols of discussing it with the whole team of ministers, and then taking the plan to the senior ministers, and eventually the full Ship Council. Instead they discussed going directly to Trendy with their plan. He and he alone would be able to champion this cause out of committee and into action.

"I don't think the others will listen," Willow said. "In fact, I believe Haddon has already thought of this plan and doesn't like it."

Scotte nodded. "Some of the deecuns are asking interesting questions too. One of them came by my desk the other day and asked me, 'Why can't we break free forward? Why do we have to go back?' I told him I didn't think it was possible. I feel bad that I lied."

"Don't feel bad, these are dangerous times we're in. You did the right thing." She looked up, and then came back with another question, "Have you told your wife?"

Scotte smiled. "I know I shouldn't have, but I couldn't help it. Stacy and I have never held secrets. She and I talked about it a couple of days ago."

"What does she think?"

"She's all for it. She can't stand Dort anyway. Before all the change happened she was pushing me to change Sundy Skul and Dort had been against it. In fact, he had stopped it. She sees this as a chance to get him out of leadership. I am worried, though, that she might not be thinking clearly. She was affected by the change in bad ways. First, there was my near death in the engine room and my injury frightened her. On top of that the parent of the baby who died is one of her ballet students. It's just been very tough for her. Things haven't worked out like she thought they would."

Willow picked up his line of thought and said, "I've been meaning to ask you this. Does it seem to you at all like, in some ways, we've all changed since this happened? I don't mean the normal change which happens in life, but, I am worried our personalities have been altered or that we're moody and mean, or maybe territorial. The spirit of cooperation and teamwork is missing."

Scotte nodded. "Yes, I think your right. Whatever is happening outside of the *Smith and Helwys* is definitely having repercussions on our interpersonal relationships. No one around here seems very Christ-like. Do you think it is changing us?"

"I don't know," Willow responded. "I don't think so. I do think it has affected Dort and Trendy. Neither one of them seem to be acting the way he used too."

"Amen," whispered Scotte.

The two talked a little more. Scotte felt relieved when he learned that Willow had told her husband, Bill, as well. They both agreed something positive must be done, and that Dort would block it. Before they left, the two prayed about the monumental decision and then committed to brief Trendy of the plan the next morning.

What neither one of the ministers knew was that just around the corner, slouching in a comfortable chair was Criswell. He had heard their entire conversation and within ten minutes he was standing in front of Dort and told him all about it, verse by verse.

B. E. Trendy was elated when he heard of Willow and Scotte's plan.

"I knew we would find our purposes in the midst of this. We must ride the wave and emerge!" He became very energetic and excited as he thought about how it would work. "In the matrices of change, it follows that all of the *Smith and Helwys* would change. Our organizational structure as well as the way we teach the seminary for children would change. Instead of teaching by disciplines, we could teach by levels of maturity." Trendy went on for quite a while.

Finally, Willow interrupted. "Minister, you must know this might not work. In fact, the other two gospel leaders might find a flaw in our plan. Once they look over our homiletics, they may find we have made a mistake."

Trendy's eyes grew serious, and somewhat diabolical. "Do not share this with anyone. Tonight we engage the engines. Stay in the engine rooms and prepare the gospels for action. Wait for my commissioning of action and be ready."

"But sir," Scotte protested. "What about the Deecuns? What about the rest of the Ship Council? What about Dort? The others must be brought in on this."

"They have been," he said. "We will," he was stammering, realizing his guard had been down. He quickly regained his composure and said, "It's just that we need to move fast. But remember, this was your idea. When I give the order, you must be ready to fire the thrusters, no matter what. Understood? Remember what Sandi Creak told us. This is about our legacy and we must be decisive."

The two ministers nodded, but were uncomfortable. They both felt very much like cogs in a much larger engine than they had imagined. There was a fog of doubt that encrusted both of them as they left Trendy's platform.

Their confusion stemmed from what they did not know. They did not know that three of the Deecuns and Fosdick were already on Trendy's side and had been preaching for a political takeover of the ship. The engineers were largely free of such political mechanizations, and so were out of the loop. Trendy knew that with this new hermeneutical information about the nature of the change stream, and the use of the gospels, he was ready to act.

All he had to do was inform Dort that things were changing onboard the *Smith and Helwys*. About twenty minutes after he had time to think and shoot off some last minute communications to his supporters, Trendy exited his platform and took the hotairlift directly to Dort's platform.

He entered his counterpart's lair noticing the damage that was still evident from the incident six months earlier. As repairs had been made systematically on the vessel, Dort had insisted that his platform be the last. As a result it was a museum of the day the accident occurred, like a forensic crime scene. Or perhaps like a memorial to the past.

It was the first time Trendy had ever been in Dort's platform, and one of the rare instances he'd ever been in engineering. Trendy was aware of how everything ran, and was conversant with the uses and capabilities of the engines, but he rarely dealt with the nuts and bolts.

"May I help you, Minister Trendy?" Dort asked the question with a lifted eyebrow and a suspicious tone.

"Yes. You can agree that I am the new leader of the *Smith and Helwys* and I will allow you to remain the chief minister of the gospels. If you don't, I'll replace you with Willow."

Dort laughed and said, "Really. What makes you think I would agree to that?"

"I happen to have new information on a plan that will propel us forward and ride the change stream to a new home. A new home God wants us to have. You, however, are standing in our way. So step aside. Allow a fresh, new vision of the *Smith and Helwys* to emerge. It would be easier if you publicly ceded any desires for the position of Paster. Don't make me bring this before the Ship Council. It would only end poorly for you."

"Perhaps," Dort admitted. "But what you don't know is that I know all about your foolish plan. What you want to do violates all the laws of what we know the universe is like. If you proceed, you will fundamentally change what it means to be a part of this vessel. It is a violation of our covenant and heritage."

"Heritage!" Trendy shouted the word with a snarl. "What does heritage have to do with anything? We are moving forward to build a new heritage for our children and generations to come. The universe changed six months ago—but you are still living in the past."

"God has predestined me for this moment." Dort truly believed what he was saying and he said it with resentful intensity. "It is God's will.

We must return to the past, to the way things used to be. The past is our guide for the future."

"No!" Trendy interrupted. The past is a hindrance, shackling us to the same broken ways. Our purpose is to move forward." Trendy kept walking slowly toward the older, slender Dort in an aggressive way. "But I am not here to discuss philosophy of ministry with you. Will you or will you not yield?"

"I will not."

"Then you are finished. Your next post will be serving fried chicken on the Potluck Deck."

"I do not think so. I have a surprise or two myself."

Dort lunged for his desk and pushed a green button. When he did, a siren blared and Dort's pre-recorded voice filled the room—and every room on board the ship. "This is an emergency. Everyone return to your duty stations or your dwelling. The *Smith and Helwys* is about to commence emergency separation procedures. The ship will divide into two sections."

"Don't!" shouted Trendy as he lunged toward the desk and for Dort's throat. "Don't ruin my dreams," he said as he squeezed Dort's throat.

Dort grabbed his very large Bible, which was sitting on the desk near the green button and smacked Trendy on the head with it. He repeatedly hit him until the larger, overweight Trendy released his stranglehold.

Trendy came to his feet and gave a roundhouse toward Dort's jaw. Of course, he missed and instead drew his own blood as his fist rammed into the bulkhead. Dort gave Trendy a push and propelled him backwards on top rubble piled across the platform.

"You'd better get to your duty station. This ship is about to separate. I'd hate for you to end up on the wrong side when it does. Who knows what my people would do to a Judas like you?"

"This isn't over," promised Trendy as he wobbled out of the room still cradling his wounded hand. He turned around for one more parting shot, "Where there is no vision the people perish, Dort. You are the most visionless man I've ever met." With that he walked to the hotairlift and pressed the number for his platform. Trendy knew that once the emergency separation procedure had begun, the ship's computer would automatically carry out the order in forty minutes.

Once he reached his platform, he keyed into the ship's communication network.

A holographic image of Minister B. E. Trendy appeared in every room on board the ship. "This is your new Paster speaking. Sy Dort has sabotaged our beloved vessel. In approximately thirty minutes the *Smith and Helwys* will separate into two of its four component parts. Before that happens, I, along with two ministers of the gospels, have a plan to get us forward toward a new home. Pray for us."

The holographic image sputtered out as Trendy finished his sermon. He pushed his other communication device which led directly to Willow and Scotte. "Willow, I am promoting you to lead Minister of the Gospels. Engage all four engines now. "

"I can't, Paster." It was hard for her to call Trendy "Paster," given what had just happened. Nevertheless, she was still committed to the action for she believed it to be for the best.

"Why?" he demanded.

"Because Haddon and Criswell have changed the key code for their gospels. We can't engage those engines."

"Paster," Scotte chimed in. "I think I know a way to bypass them. It'll take some time and might cut it close, but it just might work."

"Do it. Do it now."

"Amen, Paster," Scotte affirmed.

Meanwhile, Dort yelled down from his platform above the four gospels. He screamed to Haddon and Criswell, "Put the engines in full reverse and prepare for *Operation Breaking Glass*."

Haddon responded bluntly, "What if it doesn't work. We haven't tested it."

"It will work. This is God's will."

"Amen," said both Haddon and Criswell.

Because the engineering area was so closely configured, both Willow and Scotte heard the exchange between Dort and the two ministers loyal to him. They immediately recognized the threat. There would be no time to bypass the locked out codes because Dort's plan would happen as soon as Haddon and Criswell brought up the engines.

Willow punched in the visual communicator to Trendy. "Paster, the other two gospels are firing now under Dort's command. They are going backward. There is no time to wait for Scotte to by-pass. What

122

do you want us to do?"

"Scotte," said Trendy, as he pushed the display icon, "can you try and fire our two engines at the same time they fire theirs so that we offset their thrust. If we can force a stalemate, it might give you enough time to get their codes by-passed."

"We can try, Paster. But there are no guarantees. Right now, we are doing with these gospels things they were never designed to do."

"I understand that, Scotte," Trendy assured him. "But we must trust that the Lord is on our side."

"Amen," Willow affirmed.

Their communication ended and Willow and Scotte both prepared their engines. From his Mark engine Scotte could read the energy build-ups for Matthew, Luke and John. He glanced over his shoulder to spy Willow monitoring her Luke Engine. They were both watching their engine stations, but also watching their backs. Down inside Scotte was afraid Dort might try something violent. He couldn't worry about that, though. He focused on trying to by-pass the codes for the other gospels. Unfortunately for him, Haddon was his match and had anticipated every trick he tried. It seemed this would not work.

Suddenly a blaring announcement echoed through the ship: "Alert. The *Smith and Helwys* will separate in three minutes."

Scotte grimaced. It would be a long three minutes and his life, and the life of his family and friends depended on it. He hoped Trendy knew what he was doing. Three minutes wasn't long to contemplate a whole life. Three. Then he remembered that Jesus was in the tomb for three days but came out alive. Suddenly he burst into song, "Up from the grave he arose, in a mighty triumph o'er his foes."

Willow heard him and began to hum. It was a delightful moment of peace in the midst of terrible chaos. The peace was nice, and for the moment it felt like the old days when they were a happy crew of Baptists, not a schismatic gang on the verge of self-destruction.

Then the moment of peace ended. Haddon and Criswell finally got their engines ready and began the thrusting sequence. Simultaneously, Scotte and Willow powered up their engines to match thrust. It was the first time the engines had been used since the accident. Never, to anyone's knowledge, had the ship had half the engines firing one way and half the other.

The effect was that the ship would lurch forward, and then lurch backward, like a sea vessel lurching on the tide. Willow shouted across the deck, "Haddon, stop it, you will tear the ship apart. Don't you see?"

The irritated minister chided back, "Me? You're the one tearing the ship apart. Your mutiny will destroy us. Repent, and come back. When this is all over, we will forgive you. Can't you see, Paster Dort is right. The only way out of this is to go backward, to the old ways when things were normal."

"Amen!" chimed Criswell. "You will get us all killed."

The situation was irreparable. Neither side would or could back down. They were committed to different courses of action. Each action was justifiable and understandable, yet polar opposites. Not one of the four ministers of the gospel knew what would happen if this continued. All four of them were just wishing it would all end.

Suddenly the ship began to creak. Scotte thought the ship was beginning to fold in upon itself because of the gospel stress. But that wasn't it. It was the separation sequence Dort had started. Scotte had already forgotten about that. The *Smith and Helwys* was splitting in two. Trendy and Dort were getting what they wanted. There would be a ship split and they both will get to be Paster.

In an instant the titanium bulkhead designed to implement in separation came down right between the four control panels of the engines. On one side was Mark and Luke and on the other was Matthew and John. Willow patched in her communication device to Criswell.

"There is still time to stop this. We can all shut down our engines while the ship separates. We have no idea what will happen if we keep this thrust going during the schism. Do you hear me? Criswell?"

"I hear you. But I am not turning off my engine. I can't trust you. If I turn mine off. You will keep yours going, or worse yet, Scotte will get through and decode my gospel and fire it from his control panel. No way. I know that you are right about not knowing what will happen, especially in this constant change vortex, but I can't trust you. I'll take my chances. I wish it didn't have to be this way."

With that, he ended the communication.

The ship continued to separate. The design of the vessel was such that each deck was already space worthy with its interior wall and when it peeled off there was no noticeable difference from the interior of the ship. Only the engine room required new walls to separate the engine's room. Those walls were now on an automatic timer.

When Dort had keyed in the sequence, he had ordered a two phase separation, not a four phase. The ship literally halved itself. When it did there was a split second when the two vessels were separate but floating side by side. Then with a quick start both vessels darted out in different directions.

From his platform Trendy asked, "What happened? Willow, what is going on down there?"

"We are riding the stream, Paster, just like we thought. Mark and Luke are at full capacity."

"Amen!" shouted all the platform crew.

"What happened to the other part of us, to Dort? I hope they are okay."

"I do not know, Paster. The data we have here indicates they are not at our past location. When we shot forward, they shot backward. We do not detect any debris; given the fluctuations and variables in this part of space we just do not know."

Scotte paused for a moment and then continued.

"Paster, I think it might be nice if you said a prayer for them."

"Prayer, oh, yeah."

Scotte had meant for Trendy to make a prayer for him and Willow to share in. But that was not Trendy's first thought. Never missing an opportunity for being out in front, he keyed up the ship wide hologram. "This is Paster Trendy. Just moments ago we successfully jumped onto the change particle stream. We are riding the wave to our legacy. Unfortunately, some who were with us chose a different path. We should pray for them."

Paster Trendy then prayed, "Lord, help those who chose poorly to change their mind and join us on the change particle stream. We pray they are okay, but rejoice that you have blessed us. In Jesus Name, Amen."

Meanwhile, Willow and Scotte gathered the engineering crew for Mark and Luke and held hands and prayed their own prayer. They prayed someday they might join their friends again. They prayed that Dort and the others were safe. They prayed for wisdom. They christened the newly separated engine room of the two gospels with their salty tears.

Three months later found Paster Trendy deep in thought on his platform. He had recently remodeled his platform to include diagrams and charts of how *The Smith* was structured. He was currently pondering the organizational chart for the Potluck Deck. The original Potluck Deck had been on the other side of the separation. Therefore it was necessary to convert most of what had been the Prayer Deck into the Potluck Deck. He had spent the past week pondering the purpose of prayer. Particularly he wondered if there was a more streamlined way that would connect with people better than a whole deck of his ship dedicated to it. That space could be used more efficiently. People could pray anywhere.

"Paster," a female voice echoed out of his communications device, interrupting his thoughts. It was his Usher on the Main Pulpit.

"Yes, Driscoll, what is it?"

"Well, there is something up here I think you should see."

"What? What is it?"

"Paster," her voice stammered, "It's a ship."

"A what? I'll be right there."

Paster stood and straightened his uniform, as he always did before presenting himself to the rest of the Ship, and strode into the hotairlift. Within seconds he stepped out onto the Main Pulpit. The Main Pulpit was the command nerve of the whole vessel. It was the original Main Pulpit from the old unified vessel. Trendy had made some modest improvements, though, to its function. The Liquid Screen was made much bigger, and each station was made more user friendly. The ushering station, where navigation took place was upgraded to include up to the minute readouts of the change fluctuations outside in the change-particle wave they were riding. The committee station, where communications were filtered through, was given the pride of place with a podium right in the middle of the Main Pulpit. Trendy had issued several NFLday sermons insisting how important communications were in this new era of riding the change wave to a new home.

Trendy's eyes darted toward the Announcements station. He glared at Driscoll and said, "This better not be a prank!"

"No prank, Paster. Do you want it on screen?"

"Of course I do."

Driscoll gulped as she brought the image up. She knew he would not be happy with what he saw. Coming right at them was an exact replica of themselves.

"Is that a shadow, Driscoll?" Trendy hoped it was.

"No sir. We thought the same thing. We magnified the image and the hull markings are pretty clear."

"Let me see."

"Amen, Paster."

The image smoothly transitioned to a larger, clearer magnification which revealed the name of the vessel. It read in distinct black letters, *"The Helwys."*

Trendy stood on the Main Pulpit with his mouth wide open. Suddenly Scotte's face emerged on the liquid screen. "Paster. You will not believe this. I just received an encoded message from Haddon. He says they think they are going backward, in reverse. I told him he was crazy and that we were going forward. Yet, somehow, we've managed to bump into one another."

"Sir," Driscoll interrupted. We are getting a visual message from the Helwys. Do you want to reply?"

Trendy thought hard. This was his worst nightmare. The very presence of the other vessel in *front* of his present condition seemed to invalidate all of his preconceived ideas about the nature of this changed space. He gulped hard and said, "Yes."

Dort's image filled the giant screen. He was standing on his platform. Curiously, the first thing that Trendy recognized is that Dort still had not made repairs to his platform. The two men glared at each other through the liquid image.

"B. E. Trendy, it seems we meet again. I thought your ship was destroyed. I am, glad it wasn't. It is good to see you."

"We thought the same about you." A smile crept across his face and he had to admit, "It is good to see you as well. How are you guys holding up."

"Fairly well. How about you?"

"We are well. What has happened? How did we meet each other even though we are going in opposite directions?"

Dort explained, "Well, I wondered the same thing. It just happens that as we encountered you, Sandi Creak was on my Platform. She says God is letting us just run in circles until we figure out exactly what we're supposed to learn from the nature of change itself and not to try and manipulate it. She might be right. She also mumbled something about us acting like babies who need their milk. She might be right about that too."

"Maybe. I know I made mistakes," It was hard to admit, but Trendy knew he had behaved terribly unspiritual. However, he recognized that things were very different now. He raised his left hand and said, "But I don't think we can go back. I suggest that we point ourselves in the same direction and travel together, side by side. Maybe some day we can reunify."

"There are too many hard feelings for reunification now," Dort grimaced as he said it. "But I amen. We can certainly travel together, with each of us having our own way of doing things. Perhaps someday in the future we can be as one."

Trendy instantly had an idea. "Some of our people really miss those on the Helwys. Maybe we can arrange for some recreation time for our crews."

Dort smiled. "Yes, that would be Hallelujah."

Sermonologue

The last note on the guitar faded, and the Pastor stood up to give his Sunday morning sermon.

Open up your Bibles to 1 Peter 3.

I almost titled this sermon, "How to Tiger Proof your Marriage with Something Better than a Golf Club" but I decided that might be a little harsh. Nevertheless, what an example of an out of control marriage? I've been preaching about family now for the past couple of weeks, and today I want to get to some vital issues in marriage.

As he said the words, two very different thoughts crossed his mind. The first was incredulity that a big-time sex scandal would be about a golfer. Really! A golfer? What next, a ping pong player? Who knew golfing was that interesting. He was glad he didn't golf.

The second thought was more on task. He could see the faces that were there at church this morning. What bothered him, though, were the ones not there. It pained him to admit to himself that half of the marriages in his church were in trouble and most of the ones in trouble were not here! Somewhere Christianity has missed the mark in communicating the vital aspects of a healthy family life. He hoped his sermon would help; but history told him most people just nod and then leave the worship center unchanged and still miserable.

Last week I was talking to my mother because it was my birthday. She did what she always does. She told me all about the day I was born and the trauma involved. Apparently, pieces and parts of me tried to be born before I was actually ready. They tell me that my life as well as my mother's life was only saved because of an emergency C-section after an hour ride in the backseat of my grandmother's vehicle on icy roads.

Should he have said that? It was mildly graphic, but accurate. He thought of people who might be offended of such graphic speech during a sermon. He might get an angry letter or two over that one.

It sounds all very exciting.
The problem is, I don't remember any of it.

My mom was telling me all of this and then she indicated that a child's birthday should be when we celebrate his or her mother, not the child. I laughed and said, "Well, maybe we should work to combine birthday's and Mother's day into one great big celebration."

He thought of his mother as he said these words. Other than his wife, no human being on the planet had been more important to him. Ministry had called him to live thousands of miles from his mother and father. He wondered if he'd been a good son, how could he at such a great distance. As he told this story about his mother he thought about the fifth commandment, the one with the promise, "Honor your father and mother that your days may be long upon the earth." At the same time he thought of Jesus who said, "Who is my mother, and who are my brothers?" Christ had implied that family relations took a backseat to the Kingdom needs. It had proven to be a great tension to him. His face made a grimace as he thought of it, but he continued with the story.

Now, that took us, my mother and me, as we spoke on the phone, down the whole road of Mother's Day. Particularly we giggled about how it used to be done in churches. There might be flowers—usually three bouquets. The pastor would start the bidding, say, at six. "Are there any ladies here today who have six children or more?" Then a smattering of women would stand and he would increase it, "seven?" A few would sit down, "eight?" Another would take her seat and it would keep going until some beleaguered mother with thirteen children would be recognized as the mother with the most children. She was applauded by the congregation as a great hero of stamina and given her bouquet of roses.

How many wives over the years sat through those moments in church and smiled on the outside, but deep on the inside cried. They cried because although they desperately wanted children they were never able to have any. Not even one. Yet other women seemed to be able to procreate at will? Having many children didn't mean a woman was a good mother.

He and his wife had two boys and a girl. But then there were the two others, maybe they were both girls, he liked to think they would have been girls, which never saw sunlight. In many ways that trauma never left him; or his wife. If someone asked him how many children he had, the answer out of his mouth was three. The answer inside his heart was five.

130

Then the process would repeat itself. Do you folks remember how that worked? The preacher would begin the bidding with, "Are there any mothers here today eighty years old or older." Eventually, through the same process, the woman who was a mother and the oldest would be discovered. It was usually some dear saint in her late nineties, and almost always the same woman year-in and year-out. This was some kind of award, I think, for the stamina that your children hadn't killed you yet.

As a young boy, I always remember thinking that after church all the other women would get together and plot how they could have more babies before next year in some strange form of competitive child rearing. Isn't it odd how we honor mothers by using their children as scorecards? Clearly, it seems, men came up with this methodology.

Oh, the things I didn't know then.

Finally, there was always one more bouquet. The same procedure was taken as with the oldest mother, except it was for the youngest mother. Usually the bidding started about twenty-two. I remember the year I was a freshman in high school. The winner was in my Sunday School class.

Her name was Jennifer. Jennifer was such a popular name back then. He thought about Jennifer and wondered how she was. He would have to look her up later and find out if she was on Facebook? Jennifer was nice. She was a twirler. Or was she a cheerleader? He'd once had a crush on her, but apparently so did someone else. He tried to remember who the father of the baby was. He couldn't remember. Why couldn't he remember? Think..Think..Think. He couldn't. That bothered him. What kind of horrible man was he that he remembered the young girl who had indiscretion and lived with it, but not the young man who was just as guilty of indiscretion? It couldn't have just been her problem, yet that is what he remembered. Society was truly upside down and hypocritical. "God forgive me," he prayed deep within himself.

That might be the last year I ever saw that—we really don't want to encourage teen unwed pregnancy with flowers at church, now do we?

As we learned last week, families have always had problems and challenges. Yet obviously, the world has changed. Our question today is whether or not the Bible has anything to say that might help us in these challenging times? As you expect, I think it does.

I think in some way the Bible's pretext is not the picturesque family, but the blended, hodgepodge families facing difficulties in their relationships, just like many of us today. I have good reason to believe this.

He glanced across the sanctuary. A woman just walked in and sat down on the back row on the stage left side. She was well dressed and smiling, but alone. She was not someone he knew. He guessed her age to be about 50ish. Oh no. Here he was preaching a sermon about marriage and there is a guest who looks to be perhaps a divorcee, or life long committed single woman. Go figure. Oh well, you can't bat a thousand, he thought to himself. How long it would be before she got offended or bored and left?

People are the same basic creature today as we were two millennia ago. New Testament families didn't have it all together either. Both Paul and Peter in their letters give encouragements and strong exhortations to husbands, wives and children. That tells me a lot of these early Christian women were not exactly the dutiful wife type and apparently men were having some serious problems in their family relationships. This morning we all must remember that these were people inside the church.

My personal favorite is from Paul. He actually comes right out and tells men, "Husbands, love your wives" (Ephesians 5:25). A man's love for his wife should be the same as Christ loves his church. That is a powerful kind of love. I think it is funny that Paul has to actually tell husbands they should love their wives.

We might think that is a given yet in the world in which he lived most marriages were arranged. A couple might not meet until their wedding day; so love had to be nurtured and cultivated and worked at. This again reminds us that love is not an emotional feeling. Love is a decision to put the wellbeing of someone else above your own.

The older his children got, the more he thought arranged marriages were a good idea. Surely he and his wife knew better who his children could be happy with than they would know? With the divorce rate growing, maybe a trend back toward arranged marriages would be a good idea? Let's see, who could he pair up his daughter with? There was that boy in the preschool department who had the really good parents? What of his teenage son, though? A smile escaped his mouth as he thought about that. He felt disconnected from the words he was saying. His mind was somewhere else. He thought about how he would have resisted such a pact if his parents had tried to arrange his marriage. No, he wanted to protect his children, but he was a romantic at heart. He'd be content to let the chips fall where they may in this messy endeavor called love. God would shepherd his children to the right person. At least that is what he prayed.

And sometimes that feeling doesn't feel particularly good.

Paul wasn't the only apostle to comment on the issue. Peter does too. I want to look a little more closely at Peter's words because they help us put the pieces back together from less than perfect situations too, I think. I want to warn you before we start, some of the ideas Peter brings up may feel offensive.

Homiletical tension was beautiful. Now they might all pay attention to see if they get offended.

Especially the first one. This should be exciting, so buckle up.

He picked up his heavy leather bound Bible. In seminary he was taught that a preacher should always hold his Bible, like Charles Stanley does on television. The justification was that the Bible was a symbol of authority. As long as the preacher held the Bible, he looked and sounded more authoritarian. For years he had done just that; and gotten very comfortable with it. But recently he'd learned people were more comfortable if he put his Bible down and talked to them openly with the natural use of his hands. It had taken a little getting used too, but eventually this form of communication felt more natural to him; more conversational. Now he had his Bible on the table near the center of the chancel. He picked it up when he referred to the text, which is what he was doing in this moment.

So here we are in 1 Peter chapter 3. Find verse one. " Likewise, wives, be subject to your own husbands, so that even if some do not obey the word, they may be won without a word by the conduct of their wives, when they see your respectful and pure conduct."

The word that offends us here is "subject." We normally don't like to think of wives as "subject" to their husbands. But context is everything.

Careful preacher. Careful. He knew he had to be very careful. There are only, maybe two topics in his flavor of Christian that might be more controversial than the husband-wife relationship. He knew that some of his hearers were convinced that God intended for men to be the leader, large and in-charge of the home and that a godly wife was one that submitted to her husband. He had no desire to infuriate these people; they were good Christian people who stretched their lives over a conservative framework.

However, this particular view was not his own. Egalitarian was more the word to describe his view of men and women in the kingdom of God, and that included marriage. However, it was not something he was prepared to fall on his sword over this morning. He wanted to talk about marriage relationships. Yet he had to do some explaining before he could get there.

He sat down his Bible and began the hard work of hermeneutics. Between the Bible and the people was the hard work of interpretation.

In the ancient world it was a naturally assumed concept that the man was the ruler, the leader. The Hebrews had very misogynist ideas of women, but the Greeks were worse.

He remembered a class he had at college where he'd read Pericles say the greatest praise of a woman was to be neither praised nor spoken of negatively. The greatest praise, Pericles had said, was to not be mentioned at all.

The Romans were a little more open minded, but nothing like most people would think of open minded today. The truth is that all ancient cultures would have not even thought twice about the truth of what Peter just said. They would have simply accepted it as universal and moved on to the next issue. But as our world has changed, these are not universal any longer.

Yet Peter bathes this ancient universal proposition in Christian mission. Notice the rationalization Peter gives in verses 1 and 2. Peter is thinking about women who believe in Christ but have husbands who do not. In this scenario, a woman should defer to her husband so as to plant the seed and the image of Christ's servanthood. The goal is evangelistic. The goal is not a family values kind hierarchy. People may legitimately argue that all wives should be subject to their husbands. I don't agree, but it is a legitimate discussion. However, from this particular text Peter is really arguing that all Christian wives should be subject to their unbelieving husbands as a model of servanthood.

Whew. He'd gotten through that for now. He knew as long as he stuck to the text and made an evangelistic emphasis he would be okay. Whenever preachers get in trouble, just plead evangelism as your goal and most people will overlook anything they disagree with. Nevertheless, he glanced around and noticed two or three snarling faces, but the woman who had come in late was still there.

That Peter addresses this in a mixed marriage kind of way seems to indicate within a family of believers servanthood should flow both ways. Mutual submission should be given to one another depending upon the situation and the prompting of the Holy Spirit. It is our duty to submit to the needs of all of those within our family so our gentleness may influence them positively for Christ.

But before someone starts trying to build a complicated hierarchy within families, I need to remind you of something. Submission is a Christian virtue; period. We are to submit to each other; to authority, to Christ, to pretty much everyone. We must stop reading these passages and thinking about alpha males. This is not the Dog Whisperer in which the alpha male wants everyone to be in a submissive pose. We are not animals, but rational human beings who choose to love.

Easy. He may have just crossed a line. Many conservatives actually believe in hierarchy of family. He might have to soothe someone when this was over and convince them that he was actually a Christian.

This is one of the things love means. We put others first—ahead of ourselves. So it should be no surprise that wives should submit to their husbands. Husbands, sometimes, have to submit to their wives too.

He wished he would have been brave enough to not say "sometimes." Yet in this congregation that was a necessary qualifier.

But Peter is not to husbands yet, he gets to them later in the text. So let's spend a little more time, as did the Apostle, on women.

He picked up his Bible again.

We pick up with verse 3 and move on through four. "Do not let your adorning be external—the braiding of hair and the putting on of gold jewelry, or the clothing you wear—but let your adorning be the hidden person of the heart with the imperishable beauty of a gentle and quiet spirit, which in God's sight is very precious."

Peter is still talking to women, to wives. That is his first group of importance. I mean that. It is far more important for women to have their act together than for men, because women seem to be a much greater element to a family's success. Not to imply that men are not important, men and male influence upon children is vital. However, women seem to influence the cohesion of the family unit more.

The family needs both to be as healthy as it can be, but usually the overall health depends upon the character of the wife and mother. Peter picks up two pieces

Peter Piper picks a peck of pickled peppers

of the family unit which are vital. First, the notion that modesty in the dress of women is important for a family keeping it all together.

This is sometimes pushed too far in some Pentecostal circles. The view there is that women should never wear jewelry or that they should never have nice haircuts. I however, do not believe in keeping our women ugly.

He laughed out loud, as did his congregation. He didn't mean any harm or malice toward those old fashioned Pentecostals. In his mind he could see Oral Roberts railing and sweating. Truthfully, he admired the courage of conviction which those godly Pentecostal women demonstrated. It reminded him of how he always admired the conviction of Mormons. He just believed they were all wrong; even though they were sincere.

Who was that woman—what was her name? Linda, that's right it was Linda. Linda had been an old hardliner that had decided, for some

136

unknown reason, to become a member of his church years ago. After he baptized her she'd cut her hair and wore it short. It was a terrible act of defiance to her former Pentecostal church.

Curiously, when her hair grew back out, she quit his church and went back to the Pentecostals. Apparently, you can go home again.

This is not the intention. The intention is to make sure a wife who should be busy with life ought not care so much what persona she exudes. More to the point, a wife has no business trying to be 'sexy' for anyone other than her husband and she might want to spend the money she threw down for that big rock on her finger for something more practical, like a college fund for her daughter.

He paused. For a split second he almost veered off message and went on a riff about materialism. He'd spent all week writing a sermon he will preach next month about materialism. That might be the whole point of what Peter is getting at. Women, and men too, for that matter, jeopardize their family when they spend money on flashy, trendy things right now which should be saved or invested for the future. He'd used the diamond ring on the finger, but usually it was the latest cell phone or gaming system. He probably should have used that instead. Maybe he should tear into people who spend time with their computers instead of spending time with their children.

But he didn't take that homiletical path. He instead knew that restraint was needed. He decided to stay on target. So in his mind he moved to the next section of this particular sermon which he had planned.

Now we have to ponder, would the Apostle Peter frown upon his wife subscribing to *Vogue, Elle,* or *Young Ms*? Could Peter with a good conscience sit down with a bowl of popcorn and watch "What Not to Wear" with his wife, or even, dare I say it, "Project Runway."

He paused again. Most people in the congregation were shaking their heads. Uh Oh. They were not tracking with him. This might be harder than he thought.

Probably. Peter might have even encouraged it, especially if his wife were fashionably challenged, because I perceive Peter is not talking about fashion. There is nothing wrong or unchristian about being fashionable. What he is pointing to is that women, specifically Christian wives, ought never be guilty of valuing fashion and style over being a good parent.

Moms—help me out here…when your children are little and your trying to keep things straight, what kind of mother has time to be a fashionista? You can usually spot a mom who has her life in the right order: She is wearing sweat pants, an oversized sweatshirt or t-shirt, her hair is up underneath a hat, little or no makeup is on her face, the only jewelry is a wedding ring, her purse is the size of a gym bag and it is carrying everything from diapers to files from work, her car is filled with booster seats and she looks like she hasn't slept in days. Huh.

A mom who is doing it right often will not have the time for fashion until the kids are gone. Not that she doesn't care about it or that it is wrong. No, the issue is priorities. So Peter wouldn't mind, I don't think, if his wife escaped away to the pages of Vogue and Vanity Fair with their glossed and airbrushed models.

But I am absolutely certain Peter would not think it a good idea to subscribe to Cosmo.

One of the women who had become a close friend to him and his wife subscribed to Cosmo. That line was just for her. He thought more people would laugh at it and he was surprised they didn't.

The real point of this is the beauty of a quiet and gentle disposition. I can't say it better than that. How many families would benefit with parents—male or female, who had as their goal to be a little gentler and a lot quieter.

Kate Gosselin is not the role model for the biblically based mother. Neither is Octomom.

A friend of mine called me yesterday and told me that the Discovery Channel has a new program with Kate Gosselin and the Octomom. The show is called *The Mothers Grim*.

Of course that was another joke. Again no one was laughing. When he wrote the sermon he anticipated some humor might diffuse the tension of the subject matter. He might have to rethink that strategy if he lives to preach this particular sermon another day.

I find it curious that Peter starts with women and not men.

Now, watch this next part, it is my favorite.

He picked up his Bible and began to read.

Verse 5 says, "For this is how the holy women who hoped in God used to adorn themselves, by submitting to their own husbands, as Sarah obeyed Abraham, calling him lord. And you are her children, if you do good and do not fear anything that is frightening."

Verses 5 and 6 are my favorite. It is almost unbelievable what Peter does. He wants to support his case for a gentle, quiet, submitting wife and he drags up Sarah. Really? Sarah? This is your example Peter? Of all the women in the Old Testament, you need an example, and your go-to move is Sarah? Come on, that is absolutely unbelievable. Sarah?

Sarah, who was so modestly adorned, apparently, that not one but two Ancient Near East Kings tried to make her his concubine.

Sarah? Really.

Sarah, the woman who was so quiet that it was her idea to have her husband have sexual relationships with her servant girl because she got tired of his constant advances trying to make it happen? That was her idea, remember, not Abraham's. Although Abraham was just like Adam was in the garden. He was unable to tell his wife no.

Sarah? Really?

The Sarah who, when God showed up and promised offspring, she laughed at him. She laughed at God, and then, wait, when God called her out on it and said, why did you laugh, she denied it. She lied about laughing to God. That Sarah? That submissive, quiet, demure Sarah?

Sarah? Really?

The Sarah who was so gentle that when her servant woman named Hagar's son got to be a teenager, Sarah was so annoyed that she demanded Abraham get rid of them and cast them out into the desert. Sarah who wanted nothing to do with the baby and the baby mama? That Sarah?

Sarah? Really?

I'm telling you friends, it doesn't take very careful reading of the biblical material at all to learn there is something unique about the biblical idea, and what Peter means, when he uses Sarah as his example.

When he'd written this sermon, this was his favorite part. Particularly because he had tried to figure out exactly what it was about Sarah that Peter was thinking of? He'd rooted around some commentaries and the writings of other folks but had never come to a good conclusion. As he prayed it through, he decided to lampoon it a bit to highlight what Peter couldn't have meant. It couldn't have meant what most people assumed it meant.

Enjoyment in this section also came from one of his theological pet projects. He'd noticed that many church people were not all that well versed in the stories of the Bible. The trauma came when New Testament writers based proposition upon the assumed narrative. If people reading the text did not know the narrative, invariably their reading of the meaning would be poor or just plain wrong. By going into a little detail, although through the backdoor, he perceived he was able to stack some narrative memories inside his biblically starved hearers. He knew most people would not immediately recognize who Sarah was, or even who her husband was.

It is sometimes hard to try and discern what the ultimate message is that the Bible is telling us. But I can tell you that when Peter points to Sarah, he is not pointing to a doormat or a wallflower. Sarah was no meek woman hidden away in the kitchen far from the big important men's world. For that matter, none of the women recorded in the Bible really were.

That is because this concept is not the biblical worldview and those who spout such a worldview are not honest about the truth the Bible communicates, or they are not smart enough to think through things logically. Then there is always the lazy factor.

Oops, he'd let that slip. He didn't mean to say it, but he did mean it. Now he picked up his Bible to read the next part of the text, but he remembered where he'd been headed and needed to add one more paragraph.

In pointing to Sarah as the example, what Peter is doing is reminding us that if there were ever a wife who had good reason to quit on her husband, it might have been Sarah. He packed her up, moved her across the world, led her from one dry arid place to another and kept getting into trouble with the local boys. They were so old when God finally gave her a child, and nothing ever seemed to be easy for her. Yet she was faithful. She never quit on God, and she never quit on her marriage or her husband.

I think that is what Peter had in mind.

Now look with me at the first part of verse 7. "Likewise, husbands, live with your wives in an understanding way, showing honor to the woman as the weaker vessel, since they are heirs with you of the grace of life."

Verse 7 has so many interesting pieces in it that I want to break it up into two pieces. First, there is the 'live in an understanding way' and 'honor as a weaker vessel' thing. Peter is stating the obvious to men—women are different and have different needs and respond differently. Some men do not know that; they are surprised when their wives do not respond the way they would. So, be understanding. They are different.

But be careful, he was thinking. They are not different in a "Men are From Mars and Women are From Venus" kind of way. His experience in pastoral ministry and counseling had taught him that. That guy, what was his name...he thought to himself in the two heartbeats between words...what was his name? Well, whoever he was he was not correct in his underlying assumptions..

I have seen the weaker vessel statement so abused. It in no way means that women are defective or broken or that there is something wrong with them. To believe that is to believe God made a mistake at creation; and I refuse to believe that. Weaker vessel just means that women, usually, are not as strong physically as a man is.

His mind raced. He hadn't thought about this when writing it, but he instantly remembered a counselors meeting conducted by the military. The meeting happened when the first wave of veterans from the Iraq war were starting to come home. The military had provided a seminar on working with returning soldiers for ministers and caregivers. The seminar was good. But one of the points that was brought up was the statistic that women tend to be affected more by Post Traumatic Stress Disorder than men if both men and women were in a hostage situation. The seminar leader had asked why that was. One of the clergy there responded, "Because they are weaker vessels" and he smiled at his quick wit. The chaplain leading the seminar told him, "You are wrong sir, and I advise you never to say that again."

He went on to explain it was because in captive or hostage situations, women are invariably treated worse and abused in sexual ways.

Should he tell that story? He had time, the sermon was winding down? It would be an addition to the narrative. He surveyed the room. Immediately he counted five people who he knew with Post Traumatic Stress Disorder and suspected there were more.

No, he'd better not. It might take the focus off what he was getting at.

Let it be known, I am aware there are some women who are much stronger than most men and I am speaking generally, not specifically. For the record, whenever I come across women who could beat me up, I tend to give them exactly what they want and how they want it. Nobody gets hurt.

But we will all agree that men are usually stronger, physically, than women.

But what does that mean? A horse is stronger than me; does that mean the horse is superior? No, it's just stronger. A gorilla is stronger than me too, but I doubt a gorilla would make a very good spouse.

When he had preached this sermon earlier that morning for the 8am service, one of the men in the front row had heckled him saying, "I think a horse is way more valuable than you." It had kind of hurt, although it was only a joke. He ad libbed it into the sermon right then.

You know, this morning when I preached this Brother Ralph chimed in that he thought a horse was far more valuable than I was.

The whole congregation erupted in laughter. He made a mental note to himself to include more self deprecating humor. They seemed to enjoy making fun of him . . .

No, think it through. Peter is saying that a husband must honor his wife; not use physical power—we would call it domestic violence or physical abuse—to coerce a woman to do what you want. That is not love; that is evil, control, and power and there is no place for that in a Christian family. There is nothing more unchristian than for a man to physically exert control over a woman just because he is stronger and can. Paul tells us to love our wives as Christ loves the church. Christ never coerces or violates us. Instead he sacrifices himself and gently loves us.

142

So this piece of the family puzzle is all about husbands honoring their wives as unique and special creations of God and not lording it over them at all with their brute strength.

Verse seven ends with a curious statement. Look at it with me, " so that your prayers may not be hindered."

He had almost picked up his Bible to read it, but he didn't need to. He just quoted it.

The implication of these eight words is clear. When our families are not right and we are not behaving properly in the context of marriage our spirituality is out of kilter and it is possible that the way we treat our wife or husband means God ignores our prayers, and rejects our worship. How important is the way you treat your family? Important enough to mess up your prayer life, and that is seriously important.

Bingo! The well dressed 50ish woman sitting on stage left near the back got up and left the sanctuary. He knew he'd never see her again. If only she'd come during Lent when he was preaching the seven sayings from the cross! He figured she would end up at the Lutheran church across town. They attract baby boomers much better. They had an espresso bar.

But he needed to focus. He was now moving away from his running homily of the text and was bringing it down to some final application. The overall gist of his text was that husbands and wives should take care of one another with respect and dignity. But there was also a strong current of perseverance in the marriage relationship. He wanted to finish on that note—stick with your marriage.

So I'm working to try and figure out exactly what Peter's message for us might be. I can break it down and parse the component parts all day, but what I really must know is the point of it all. What is the message? Two thousand years ago he was writing to families stressed by persecution. But what might his words mean to families today stressed by the many fractures in our relationships: divorce, distance, death.

I wrestled with this quite a bit because the connection is not readily apparent. But a memory came to my mind. Over the holidays I read Mitch Albom's new book "Have A Little Faith." It is really good and I highly recommend it. But as I meditated on Peter's words this week I remembered another book Albom wrote three or four years ago called, "For One More Day."

He didn't care what anyone else said; he really liked all of Mitch Albom's little books. They seemed to connect naturally the physical world of everyday troubles with the spiritual side of things. Yes, they were sappy and not overtly Christian, but did that make them any less compelling?

The plot of that book is that a run down man who was making a mess of his life was miraculously visited by his deceased mother. She stayed with him, haunting him as a ghost all day long in the small town he grew up in. He got one more day with mama. Most of that day she spent telling him what a mess he was making of himself.

Isn't that what mothers are for? God love-em.

He liked the symmetry of the sermon this morning. He had started by talking about his mother. Now he was talking about someone else's mother. He didn't know if anyone else would pick up on that bowtie or not. He liked it.

Well, as the day wound on with his mother she began to ask about his marriage. Of course, his marriage was disintegrating and on the verge of ending. She told him that marriage was hard work.

Duh!

But the advice she gave to help him in that work is something close, I think, to what Peter is getting at. She told her messed up son something to the effect of, "You have to love your spouse, but you have to love your marriage too. By marriage, I don't mean the other person, but the idea of being married, the thing created by your bond. You have to love it almost as much as you would another person."

Bringing the book with him to quote from it and read the section would have been better than merely summarizing and alluding to it. But since he'd preached a homily style with so much reading already, he'd made the decision not to bring in another book. But reading books in his sermon was one of his favorite devices. It felt right and it felt somewhat artsy, or as artsy as he can be.

I don't know where Albom heard that and lifted it for his book, but he's right. That is what Peter is telling us too. Love your spouse—yes, but you have to love the life you're making too.

Wives—you have to love that this man is your husband and the idea of being his wife as much as you love that stinky old man.

Husbands—you must love having that woman as your wife, in the wife-ness of it all as much as her as a person.

Outside my front door, just to the right of the doorbell, is a wooden plaque that hangs. On that plaque is an etching of pious praying hands. Below the praying hands are the words, "The Family that Prays Together Stays Together." I've had that plaque for years. This is the third home it has hung on. It means a lot to me, mostly because I believe what it says.

Praying hands was bought at a garage sale from the Spring family. The Spring family was a pillar family in the first church he'd ever pastored. Bill Spring was a deacon who had gone into poor health. He'd buried him in that old cemetery in the hill country. He bought the plaque before the man died, but after his death it came to mean more to him. He didn't have many things from those first early years in his ministry. That was one of the few.

I believe praying together helps our family stay connected. We work at it and try to pray as a family every night with evening devotions. Sometimes we miss, but we are probably at 95% success rate at family prayer.

I also let it hang there because it gives me something to talk about when the Mormons come and knock on my door. Mormons must be trained to spot things like that because they always bring it up. It is when they discover that I don't think much of the god they pray to that the conversation generally goes south. But I like Mormons, they are always fun to talk with and I've never met a rude one.

But as I was preparing to begin this four part series on family issues to start the year, I started thinking about the saying on that plaque. It seems to indicate that prayer is the key to keeping it together; and that keeping it together—staying together, is in some level, a successful family.

I think that is at least part of what Peter is telling us this morning.

Epilogue

Dear reader, I want you to know as you finish this book how much I appreciate you reading it. As I have written, edited, and re-written parts of it over the last two years my prayer has been that something in it might inspire and encourage you in your walk through life with Jesus. Whether a line of poetry or a narrative about leadership in church, I want you to take something away which will help or perhaps stir thought. I don't even mind if you argue with me. I usually argue with every book I read in some way or another. Those are the ones I usually enjoy most.

Art, in all its forms, is always one soul longing to connect with another. In this bit of art, my heart is for pastors and leaders of faith communities. I believe deeply the greatest sermons preached are by men and women who each week, stands before the same group of people, and attempts to make sense of our world in the light of Scripture. The great majority of these people are anonymous and unheralded. Their anonymity or lack of acclaim adds to their greatness.

Likewise, the greatest pastoring is done by those people who serve the hurting and help the dying as well as instruct fellow pilgrims along the pathway toward Christ. Tonight, before you sleep, say a prayer for your pastor. When you next worship, give him or her a hug and say something encouraging. Your pastor or priest will love you for it, and probably need it. I have been so deeply blessed to serve in a loving community which constantly affirms and supports me in this way. I wish everyone had it!

Again, thank you for reading and sharing the echoes of my soul.

Breinigsville, PA USA
13 May 2010
237988BV00002B/1/P